W9-BUG-895

Large Print Stu
Stuart, Matt, 1895-
Deep hills

3558

WITHDRAWN

STACKS

NEWARK PUBLIC LIBRARY
NEWARK, OHIO

GAYLORD M

Also by Matt Stuart in Large Print:

Bonanza Gulch
Dusty Wagons
Gun Law at Vermillion
Range Pirate
Saddle-Man

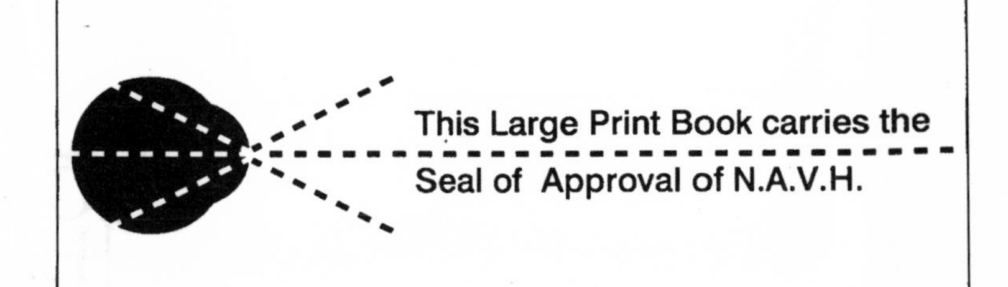

Deep Hills

Matt Stuart

G.K. Hall & Co. • Waterville, Maine

Copyright, 1949, 1954, by L. P. Holmes

A condensed version of this novel appeared in *West Magazine.*

All rights reserved.

Published in 2001 by arrangement with Golden West Literary Agency.

G.K. Hall Large Print Paperback Series.

The text of this Large Print edition is unabridged.
Other aspects of the book may vary from the original edition.

Set in 16 pt. Plantin by Warren S. Doersam.

Printed in the United States on permanent paper.

Library of Congress Cataloging-in-Publication Data

Stuart, Matt, 1895–
Deep hills / by Matt Stuart.
p. cm.
ISBN 0-7838-9488-0 (lg. print : sc : alk. paper)
1. Ranchers — Fiction. 2. Large type books. I. Title.
PS3515.O4448 D44 2001
813′.52—dc21 2001024442

Contents

Chapter I	Fandango!	7
Chapter II	Man Size	27
Chapter III	Promise of the Earth	46
Chapter IV	Dark Tides	65
Chapter V	Grim Fruit	90
Chapter VI	Tangled Trails	113
Chapter VII	The Works of Man	131
Chapter VIII	Alliance	150
Chapter IX	Time and Tension	173
Chapter X	Crimson Night	190
Chapter XI	Fruits of Toil	212
Chapter XII	Deep Hills	228
Chapter XIII	The Healing Touch	248

NEWARK PUBLIC LIBRARY
NEWARK, OHIO 43055-5087

Large Print Stu
Stuart, Matt, 1895-
Deep hills

6797477

Chapter I

FANDANGO!

THE MUTTER of hoofs became a swiftly closing rush down the dark timber road. Len Revis twisted in his saddle to listen, then said, "Running S. Hell-for-leather as usual, Britt. They'll ride us down."

As he spoke, Len was reining over to the side of the road. Britt Larkin said, "Don't do that, Len. Never give more than half of the trail to Jesse Schell. If you do, on the next pass he'll push you completely out in the brush. You ought to know Jesse that well by this time."

On either hand the timber lifted in black walls, with only the ragged crests of it silvered by the starlight, a cold radiance that did not reach the full depth of the road. The head-long approach of the Running S sent the echoes tumbling out ahead of them. Swinging back beside Larkin, Len Revis murmured drily.

"Never could see any profit in fooling around in front of any kind of a stampede. There's easier ways to die."

Britt Larkin laughed. "Horses don't run as blind as cattle, Len. Nor," he added as an afterthought, "as humans."

The tumult of hoofs coming in behind, funneled swiftly closer. Then there was a wild lunging and rearing and a hard, startled cursing as riders, some of them almost thrown by the sudden checking and dodging of their horses, fought the animals for control.

A voice lashed out, a quick, pushing note of temper in it. "You damn fools deaf? You want all the road?"

Britt Larkin answered. "Just half of it, Jesse. Our half."

"Larkin!" exploded that heavy voice. "Might have known it."

Out of the tangle of Running S riders a heavy figure came pushing. Even in this velvet dark Jesse Schell was large and thrusting and impressive with his thick thewed physical bulk. "As long as we're here," he growled, "there's a question. You heading for the valley?"

"The road leads down, doesn't it?"

From the dark tangle of the riders came another voice, hard and metallic. "Damn his mealy-mouthed palaver! Make him give you a straight answer, Jesse. Yes or no!"

Instantly Britt Larkin was pushing his horse toward the voice. His words whipped out coldly.

"Obe Widdens. When you talk tough, Widdens, come out where a man can see you!"

Jesse Schell spun his horse to block Britt

Larkin's way and yelled harshly. "Shut up, Obe! Keep your jaw out of this. When I want talk from you I'll let you know."

"You should teach your dog better manners, Jesse," Larkin said. "Damn a cur that does its snarling from the dark."

There was a placating note in Jesse Schell's growl. "Let it lay, Larkin, let it lay! Now here's the point. There's talk going around that those sod-busters down along the river flats are aiming to throw a party tonight, a fandango to celebrate their arrival in the promised land. You going to take it in?"

"What makes you think I might be?"

"For one thing, you wouldn't sign those warning notices with me and Alec Creager, telling the squatters to stay out of Reservation Valley. Maybe you like that breed of vermin. I think so."

"Well," said Larkin coolly, "having made up your mind on that point, where does it leave you, Jesse?"

Jesse Schell's dark temper began to flame again. "It leaves me telling you to stay away from them, if you know what's good for you. Alec Creager and me are calling on that outfit tonight, and if you're in the way you'll get pushed out of it."

Larkin's reply was almost casually soft. "Jesse, I'll go where I please and choose the friends that I please, not asking permission from you or Alec Creager or anybody else. That understood?"

Schell was silent for a moment. "We'll see," he

said. Then he leaned forward and sunk in the spurs and his horse, grunting under the punishment, surged away. His men exploded after him. An arm flicked out, touching Britt Larkin's hat, nearly knocking it off. Then Larkin and Len Revis were alone, the tang of churned up dust in their nostrils.

Len Revis murmured, "Now I suppose that does it. It was to be town for us and the mail and maybe a quiet, two-bit limit game of stud. But I got the feeling that meeting up with Jesse has changed all that."

Larkin settled his hat into place again, and his words ran terse. "It has. You can take care of town. I'll be stopping off at Beaver Flats."

"Knew it," mourned Len. "Boy, you can't kick every dog that snarls in the dark. Let 'em yap."

Larkin put his horse to a jog. "If you stand for their yapping long enough, they might get bold enough to try a bite."

The progress of the Running S was just a fading echo now, drifting back up from the long timber slope. Presently it was gone entirely. The road dropped down, twisting and winding, then running arrow straight across a benchland into the open country beyond. This freedom achieved, it relaxed into a casual looping across the open slopes to the final valley flats.

Here the starlight became real, flooding the valley with silver. Lights winked up from Beaver Flats. Fires were burning down there, a rough circle of them.

"Looks like that fandango is already underway," said Len Revis. "Could be a mite premature, that celebration. Now that I recollect, you ain't had much to say about that squatter camp, Britt. I'm wondering what you're thinking."

"Why, among other things, that they're a long way from the high parks we call home, Len. They'll never bother us."

Len Revis, a high, gaunt figure in the saddle, shrugged his skepticism. "You can never tell. Squatters is like the itch. They spread."

This was Reservation Valley, lonely under the wide night sky, heavily pelted all across its miles with a deep growth of sage brush, except for some grass flats along the Saber River, and of these the largest, Beaver Flats, stretched along the eastern run of the river. Here burned the fires of the squatter camp.

Ten miles west along the river were pin points of other lights, where stood Fort Cord, once a military post, but now a weather beaten little cow town, fed by a stage and freight road which ran south for two hundred miles to the railroad at Button Willow. North lifted the Royale Mountains, terraced with timber, yet holding also long running, richly grassed high parks where cattle fed and fattened.

When the road reached the flats, Britt Larkin reined in again. "Along with picking up the mail, Len, locate Hack Dinwiddie and tell him we're tolding our cavvy for that shoeing chore. Tell him I'd like to see him up at the ranch within the next couple of days, if possible."

"Just as you say. But I still think it would pay us to set up our own forge and shoe our own broncs."

A faint humor came out of Larkin. "Hack's got a right to make a living too, you know. Unless you watch out you'll be as bad as Alec Creager and Jesse Schell, figuring nobody else has any rights but themselves."

"What's wrong with trying to save money?" retorted Len. "But what I'm really concerned about is you, prowling around that fandango. You'll stick your nose into trouble, sure."

"No trouble there, Len."

"There will be," warned Len darkly. "Jesse Schell and Alec Creager will see to that. Town can wait. You better let me shag along with you."

Larkin grinned in the dark. "You're getting worse than an old woman. You go to town and see Hack Dinwiddie. If you're still worried, you can stop on your way back."

Larkin spun a cigarette into shape as he watched Len Revis disappear into the star haze. Then he swung his horse and headed off through the sage toward those winking fires by the river. Here the sage was high and thick. This was good land. It took good land to grow sage brush this size. But how could such land be brought fully into use unless the brush was cleared? And who would ever clear the brush except men like those squatters yonder? These, Larkin mused, were thoughts which Alec Creager and Jesse Schell might well play with but probably never would.

As he broke from the sage into the clear of the river flats, the sound of merry-making reached him. A fiddle was singing and a banjo tumping. Some of the younger folk were already dancing, not at all mindful that under foot lay only earth instead of a sanded floor. Older folk were grouped about, clapping their hands in time to the music beat, adding their voices to the chant of the caller. Children skylarked at play in the half-light, half-dark where the night and the fire glow came together. Wagons stood about and there were horses chomping at wild hay, stacked against the wagon wheels. Off to one side several women were tending a glowing fire pit and the savory smell of roasting meat was in the air.

For some time Britt Larkin sat his horse in the gloom beside a wagon, unnoticed. Then a couple, arm in arm, broke from the circle of dancers and headed for the fire pit. The man's quick eyes picked out Larkin's motionless figure. He stopped, said something to his feminine companion in a low tone, then stepped forward.

"Looking for somebody, maybe, cowboy?" His tone was neither hostile nor friendly, just flat and terse.

"No," answered Larkin. "Nobody. Just looking on."

"Maybe what you see don't no way please you?"

"Wouldn't say that. I like to see people happy."

The squatter was startled. "Why then," he said, "you're welcome to step down and join us. Nothing we folks would like better than to be friends with the cattle interests in this country."

For a moment Larkin neither answered nor moved. Then he swung from his saddle and put out his hand. "Larkin's the name. Britt Larkin."

"Ah!" came the murmured answer. "Luke Filchock said you might not be too hard to get along with. He named only you, though. It's Partee here, Cass Partee." The squatter's handshake was solid. "Leave your bronc here and come meet some of the folks."

Cass Partee's feminine companion stood where he had left her. Now, as he led Larkin over to her he said, "Meet Rose Calloway. Rose, this is Britt Larkin."

Her features were indistinct in the gloom, and her voice was low and grave as she spoke a greeting. Somehow Larkin knew that she would be pretty. She moved with a strong grace as she took Cass Partee's arm and walked between them over to the fires.

No sooner did Larkin come fully into the light than a murmured stirring ran through the night. The clapping of hands ceased, the chant of the caller died abruptly, the dancers stilled and the music ran out and stopped on a high, off-key fiddle note.

A blocky, bearded man said, "I knew it was too good to last." He moved over to face Larkin, his eyes burning. "Now, I suppose, we're about to hear the same old story. We can't stay here because this is cattle range, controlled by such-and-such an outfit, which makes us trespassers in the eyes of the law. And we are still worms and have no rights, so we must wiggle on. Yeah, the same old story we've heard so many times before we're sick of it. Only this time it could be different. Maybe we're not moving on. Maybe this time we're staying!"

The girl, Rose Calloway, said, "You're jumping at conclusions, Father. I don't believe Mr. Larkin feels that way about us."

Oake Calloway laughed scoffingly. "If he doesn't, daughter, then he's the first. I'll have to hear him say it."

Larkin looked around. The squatters were slowly gathering on all sides of him, first the men, then the women. Even the kids sensed the change and their shrill voices quieted. Larkin brought his glance back to Oake Calloway.

"So far as I know," he said quietly, "this land belongs to no one except the Government and is open to homesteading. It is part of the old Fort Cord military reservation, long since abandoned. You people have as much right to it as anybody. And don't let anyone tell you it's good cow country as it stands, for it's not. The sage is too thick and heavy. There's no room for grass to grow, except along the river flats and there's not even enough grass there to warrant bringing a herd down out of the high parks of the Royales to pasture on it. So, if I were in your boots," he ended, placing each word distinctly, "I'd dig in right here and I wouldn't let any man push me out!"

A murmur ran around the listening group. Oake Calloway stared at Larkin with pinched down eyes as he spoke bluntly.

"Those are words I never expected to ever hear from the lips of any cattleman. You make it sound almost as though we were welcome, Larkin. And I know better. We're not."

Larkin shrugged. "You are as far as I'm concerned. I got no quarrel with you people. But I warn you, I'm speaking only for myself. There are sure to be others who will feel differently. Now, I didn't mean to break up your fun. I'll get along."

He turned back toward his horse, but Cass Partee caught him by the arm. "I invited you to join us, Larkin. That meat smells like it was about ready. You'll stay and eat with us. Any objections, Oake?"

Oake Calloway showed hesitancy, did not answer. A man in the circle spoke for him. "That feller ain't our kind at all."

Cass Partee turned on the speaker. "Day in and day out I've heard you men curse cattlemen, damning them for all our troubles, yapping because they never showed us the friendly side of their hand. Yet, here is one who does, and you want to run him out of camp. What the devil's the matter with you, anyhow?"

Partee turned back to Oake Calloway. "Let's have an answer, Oake. You got any objections?"

Calloway measured Larkin again with narrowed glance, then shook his head. "No. No, I guess not."

"Well I have," said a harsh, nasal voice. "I'm not too sure this feller ain't a spy, sent down here by them damned cattle outfits in the mountains to look us over good and see how many there are of us, and mebbe how many guns we got. Like Oake Calloway says, he's spoke things I never expected to hear from any damn cowman. And I find 'em hard to believe."

The speaker came pushing up beside Oake Calloway and now stood there, gaunt, long-faced, bitter. Something little short of outright hatred blazed in the glance he laid on Larkin.

Larkin's face hardened. "I'm not used to being called a liar. But I'll let it pass this time, all things considered. I can see that you'll enjoy yourselves better without me around."

He pulled away from Cass Partee's hand and headed back for his horse. Cass Partee followed him.

"Sod Tremper's not speakin' for the rest of us, Larkin. He's just a bitter old devil, though maybe he can't be blamed for that, either. Cattle interests killed his son, back in the Rubicon

Plains nester-cattleman war. And his wife didn't last long after that. I'm sorry as hell about this, Larkin. I know you're sincere."

Instinctively, Larkin liked this young nester, this Cass Partee. There was something rugged and straight-forward about him. The thin edge of anger that had formed in Larkin, now ran out of him.

"That's all right, Partee. No hard feelings. In that old fellow's boots I'd probably feel the same as he does, maybe worse."

Larkin went into his saddle as he spoke, but he did not rein his horse around. Instead, he stood high in his stirrups, leaning forward a little, listening. From down along the dark flats to the west came the muffled trampling of hoofs.

"If I'm guessing right," said Larkin curtly, "old man Tremper is liable to have real cause for hating somebody before long. Quick, Partee! Get out among your people. Tell them not to start anything, even if they're pushed around some. Tell them to hold on to their tempers. I'll try and handle things."

Cass Partee hurried off, Larkin pulled his horse deeper into the shadow of a wagon and waited there.

The approaching hoofs came on at a trot, then slowed to a walk and finally to a stop as the mounted group came into the reflected glow of the fires. In the lead was Jesse Schell, blonde and burly. Beside him was Alec Creager, harsh jawed and frosty browed. These two Larkin had expected to see, but not the third leader of the group, riding close beside Creager. And at sight of her, Larkin knew a swift gust of anger.

How big a damn fool could Alec Creager be, letting Joyce ride with him on an errand like this? For here was a situation that could easily explode into violence. Jesse Schell, being the sort he was, might try and force a showdown with the nesters this very night. And if that should happen, it would be no place for a girl like Joyce Creager.

If Joyce was considering this possibility, she gave no sign of it. She sat quiet and straight in her saddle, dark head turning slightly as she glanced here and there with a cool, almost impersonal indifference. Just like she was looking at some inferior breed of animals, Larkin thought. A viewpoint garnered from her father's teachings. Yeah, all Alec Creager's fault.

Behind the Creagers and Jesse Schell were a number of cattle hands, most of them Running S, the others of Creager's Three Link outfit. At the far end of this line was Obe Widdens, lank and loose, his hat as usual riding far back on his bony head, his eyes hard and glittering with anticipation of rough mischief against these squatter folks.

There was an instinctive bunching up of the squatters, then out of this group stepped the solid, steady figure of Oake Calloway, his deep voice booming.

"Come for talk or trouble, friends?"

Jesse Schell sat his saddle solidly, not answering just now, while his glance swung back and forth and up and down the full length of the camp. Here, thought Larkin, was an example of the arrogance of the man. Schell let the tension build and thicken before he finally settled his attention on Oake Calloway.

"It all depends," he said harshly. "I'll talk and you'll listen. If you listen real close and are guided well by what you hear, there won't be any trouble. But that trouble, if it should be necessary, is right here and looking you in the eye. And you can forget that final word, because it's the wrong one. We're not, and we won't ever be friends."

Even at this distance and in the deceptive light, Larkin could see the dark blood burn in Oake Calloway's leathery face. Jesse Schell's tone and words were as cutting as a whip lash. Calloway shrugged.

"All right. Have your say."

"You seem to be celebrating something," said Jesse Schell, heavy mockery in his voice. "What it could be I can't guess. Well, you've got this night to get it out of your systems. For in the morning you'll be moving on. East or west or south, I don't care which. But you're getting out of Reservation Valley. All of you. You can't kick about this. You had your warning. You saw warning signs, telling you this land wasn't open to settlement. Seems you don't believe what you read. Well, you better believe what you hear. In the morning, you travel! And now I'm interested in that beef I smell cooking. I'm wondering whose beef? Widdens, go down to that fire pit and bring me the hide — if there is a hide. And there better be!"

Something like this was all that Obe Widdens had been waiting for. He lifted his horse to a run, deliberately cutting so close to the group of squatter folks, a gaunt woman had to snatch a big eyed, scared youngster to her to keep the child from being ridden down. Widdens peeled his lips back in a soundless, wolfish laugh.

The next moment he had to set his horse back on its haunches to avoid collision with a rider who came darting out from the shadow of a wagon. And Britt Larkin was saying, "Let's not get careless, Obe. Let's not get rough! You go on back where you came from and see that you ride damn careful while you go!"

For a long moment Obe Widdens did nothing but sit his dancing horse, too startled to think. Then his eyes took on the flat shine of something cornered. His right hand seemed to hang in the air.

Larkin laughed, but there was no humor in the sound. "What you waving at, Obe? That don't mean a thing, and you know it. You never went all the way in your life when the other fellow was looking at you."

Larkin pushed his horse closer and flipped out a reaching arm. Obe's hat spun off his head.

"Your own little trick, Obe," mocked Larkin.

"Only better done."

He kept his horse crowding in, forcing Obe's to give ground. And while Obe Widdens might have wanted to try many things, just now he dared none of them. For there was a challenge in Larkin's eyes which whipped him. All Obe did was to show a snarl and that flat, hard glare.

Then Widdens' badgered horse whirled of its own account and Larkin, snatching his quirt, lashed the animal across the haunches. The horse exploded in a wild leap and for the next moment or two all Obe Widdens could do was fight to stay in the saddle. By the time he fought his mount under control he was pretty much back where he started from. And Britt Larkin, moving ahead, was facing Jesse Schell and Alec and Joyce Creager.

"Well, Jesse," said Larkin, "here you are and here I am. Alec, how are you? Evening, Joyce. I thought you'd come to welcome these folks to Reservation Valley. Am I wrong?"

Alec Creager stared at him, fuming. "You just played the fool, Larkin. Don't be a bigger one, talking like that!"

Larkin smiled faintly. "Could be a difference of opinion there, Alec."

The old temper leaped up in Jesse Schell, hot and naked. "Back along the hill road I warned you, Larkin. I told you then —"

"You can't tell me anything, Jesse," cut in Larkin. "When are you going to get that through your head? When are you going to learn that as far as I'm concerned you own just half the trail, not one damned inch more?"

The heavy cords in Schell's throat swelled and his voice ran a little thick. "I can push you clear out of the Royales, Larkin. I can —"

Larkin cut in again, coldly blunt. "You really think so, Jesse, then now's as good a time as any to start!"

Jesse Schell stirred restlessly, as though readying himself to accept Larkin's challenge. But Alec Creager, seeing something in Larkin that was poised and dangerous, spoke up quickly.

"Steady, Jesse! This ain't helping our purpose a bit. Let's not make it a pair of fools, where one is already too many. Larkin, I want a talk with you."

"Later, Alec — later! Right now I'm waiting for Jesse to make up his mind. He jumps, or he doesn't jump. Which is it going to be, Jesse?"

A voice behind Larkin, Cass Partee's voice, said, "Just to straighten out any question about the beef we got in the fire pit, here's the hide. Also a bill of sale. We bought the beef from Luke Filchock. Take a look!"

Cass Partee dropped a green steer hide on the ground where the firelight shone on it. He spread it out. Plain to see was Luke Filchock's Box F brand.

"You don't have to show anybody anything, Partee," said Larkin.

"We don't want trouble," said Cass Partee quietly. "We'll go a long way to avoid trouble."

"Then you'll travel a long way from Reservation Valley," exploded Jesse Schell.

Larkin waited for Partee's answer to this. Maybe he'd made a fool of himself, going out on a limb this way for these squatter folk. If they caved in on him now — !

"That," said Cass Partee steadily, "is something we're not going to do. We're staying."

Oake Calloway's voice boomed. "When Partee says that, he's talkin' for all of us. Yeah, we stay!"

"Hell you are!" yelled Jesse Schell. "I can ride you down. I can — !"

"Shut up, Jesse!" said Larkin. "Right now you're riding nobody down."

"Yeah, Jesse, take it easy," put in Alec Creager. "That wild talk don't mean a thing."

While this had been going on, Alec Creager had been studying the squatter camp. After their first grouping, the people had begun to separate, drift apart. Men were herding women and children out of the way and behind the shelter of wagons. Now these same men were standing in the shadow of the wagons and by the way they handled themselves and the way they waited in grim watchfulness, Creager knew that they had picked up weapons and were ready to use them should things break that way. Jesse Schell's blindly arrogant anger could push matters into a bloody shambles. A crackle came into Alec Creager's voice as he spoke again.

"Jesse, take your men and go on home. You're

in no fit mind to reason common sense tonight."

Schell whirled on him. "You, too? I'll be damned if — !"

"Go on home," ordered Creager again. "I'm telling you, Jesse!"

Schell glared around, burly shoulders hunched forward. Larkin watched him with a thin alertness, waiting for the explosion he was sure would come. So, he was frankly amazed when Schell spun his horse, sunk home the spurs and surged away.

His men followed him, Obe Widdens riding with his round, bony head twisted, giving Britt Larkin a final malignant glance.

Larkin listened to the departing hoofs then looked at Alec Creager. "That was showing good judgment, Alec. Don't tell me you've had a change of heart?"

"Not one damned bit! But I got some common sense. I was heading off something that could have turned bad."

"Only," reminded Larkin, "if you and Jesse wanted it so. If this thing ever gets bad, it will be for the same reason."

Larkin twisted in his saddle, looked over the silent, watching squatter folk. "Partee, I'll be around to see you in the morning. Some things I want to talk over with you."

"I'll be here," was the quiet answer. "We all will. Luke Filchock said you were a thoroughly white man."

Now it was Rose Calloway who moved up

beside Partee. She looked at Larkin, a slow, gentle smile on her lips.

"Thank you," she said softly.

Her hair was tawny as ripe wheat and her eyes reflected the smile on her lips. She had lived close to the sun, this girl, and its warm quality lay in the clean curve of her cheeks and throat.

Larkin nodded gravely as he touched his hat. "That makes it worth while," he said.

He turned to Alec Creager. "If you still want to habla — ?"

Creager jerked a crusty nod. "Come on!"

Joyce Creager did not immediately follow her father. She lifted her reins, but held her horse steady while for a long moment she stared at Rose Calloway. It was a measuring glance which could have held many thoughts. Then, abruptly, she spun her mount and moved into the night.

Chapter II

MAN SIZE

THEY RODE away from the squatter camp for a good quarter of a mile without a word being spoken before Alec Creager pulled up and turned to the Three Link riders who followed.

"If you boys want to spend a few hours in town, fly to it."

The riders, only too glad to agree, spurred away. Britt Larkin got out his smoking and twisted up a cigarette, thinking that Joyce Creager's bared, dark head took on an almost silver shine under the glow of the stars.

Alec Creager cleared his throat. "This won't take long. Larkin, just why do you persist in making a damn fool of yourself? You want to start gunsmoke rolling across this range?"

"First," said Larkin quietly, "let's chop out some of that and throw it away, Alec. If you were smiling when you said it, I wouldn't mind. But the way you said it, I don't like it. You know what I mean."

Creager made a gesture of irritation. "All right

— all right. I take it back. Just the same, it was a fool stunt to brace Jesse the way you did back there."

Larkin blew thin smoke at the stars. "Don't agree. Somebody had to tell him off, so I did. About gunsmoke, no. I've no liking for it."

"You didn't act so," said Creager. "If I hadn't happened to be along with Jesse, there's no telling what would have happened."

Larkin shrugged. "Gunsmoke or no gunsmoke, I don't crawl in front of that fellow. He takes himself to be a great man. He's not. He is," added Larkin deliberately, "a pig-headed, overbearing, loud mouthed coyote! As you'll come to realize, one of these days."

"That's pretty strong talk," snapped Creager. "I'm wondering if you ever said as much to his face?"

For the first time, Joyce Creager spoke, her voice tight. "It's easy to talk behind another man's back."

In the dark, Larkin's face went hard and a sardonic note came into his words. "I thought I showed Jesse pretty much what I thought of him tonight. If he still doesn't understand my sentiments, then I'll see that he does, next time I meet up with him. That should satisfy everybody."

Larkin stirred his horse slightly, as though preparing to ride off.

"Hold it!" said Creager. "I'm not through. You made a play tonight, Larkin, that I can't figure out. We'll concede you got no use for Jesse

Schell. That's your privilege, just like it's mine and Joyce's to value him as a friend. At least we know where he stands. What I want to know is this. Did you take that stand back there tonight because you've fallen in love with a flock of damned squatters, or just because you wanted to raise a fuss with Jesse and me?"

"Not entirely the first," answered Larkin carefully. "Though there are some of those folks it wouldn't be at all hard to like. And not all of the last, either. I never have and never will want a fuss with you, Alec. But as for Jesse Schell, well, that's something else."

"I find you a little hard to understand, Larkin. You never shaped up as a particularly tough hand before. Yet back there you were covered with bristles."

Larkin shrugged. "A man can get tired of being pushed around by a lot of strut and bullypuss."

"Well, it was a damned poor spot to make your stand," said Creager. "It ain't going to help our cause any, advertising a fuss between ourselves right in front of those squatters."

"Our cause?" murmured Larkin. "Just what is our cause, Alec?"

"Why, the cause every sensible cowman believes in and sticks to. Keep any and all squatters on the jump and never let 'em light."

Larkin crushed out his cigarette butt on his saddle horn. "Then I guess I'm just not sensible."

Creager stood high in his stirrups, staring at

Larkin. "By that I take it you're not aiming in any way to help get rid of that gang?"

Larkin nodded. "You take it right, Alec. Now this will put your roach on end. I'm glad to see the squatters there. I hope they stick. Because if they do they can do me a lot of good. You, too, if you'd just open your mind a little."

"Now," rapped Creager, "I know you're crazy. I always did figure you as being a little light of weight, but I never thought you quite this bad. Jesse was right, all along. He said we could never depend on you in a deal like this."

"Jesse would say that," murmured Larkin sardonically. "Wise man, Jesse."

Joyce Creager now reached over and tugged at her father's arm. "Why do you bother to argue with him, Dad? You're just wasting your breath. He stood up for the squatters tonight, didn't he? That should tell you all you want to know."

Larkin had been trying to take this thing in stride, knowing that he and Alec Creager could throw this thing back and forth all night and still reach no convincing end. For Creager was as set as granite in his way, while Larkin had reasons for his own position which Creager would never understand. But these words of Joyce stung him and he turned on her.

"What would you have had me do back there, stand by and let that damned Obe Widdens ride down one of those women or kids? Or crawl for Jesse Schell? Well, in one way you're right, Joyce. I'll side with a decent squatter any time before I will with a pair like Jesse Schell and Obe Widdens. Now just to show you I can be as fair as the next, if your father can show me one way those people have hurt him, or ever will, then I'll go back to the flats and run them out myself."

"Joyce is right," growled Creager. "There's no use arguing this any further. I just wanted to be damned sure where you stood, Larkin. Now I know."

"A man has to stand where he thinks he's right," said Larkin. "You and Schell are stone blind on this squatter question, Alec, but for different reasons. You feel as you do because you believe that's the way a cattleman should feel toward squatters. Jesse Schell feels the way he does because he likes to kick people around, likes to see them cringe or crawl. Don't let him lead you into something you'll be sorry for, Alec."

"I'm capable of taking care of myself and my affairs, thank you." Creager was stiff and distant now. He turned to his daughter. "We'll be riding now, Joyce."

Larkin touched his hat. "Good night, folks."

Neither answered him as they rode away.

Larkin sat his saddle quietly. He built and lit another cigarette. The glow of the sulphur match, as he held it cupped in his hands, picked out the lean, brown planes of his face, fashioning them into a tight lipped, bronze mask. There was a certain storminess of feeling in his eyes.

He didn't want things to be this way between

the Creagers and himself. He had always valued the good opinion of Alec Creager. And Joyce, well, she was something very special. He still valued their good opinion. But not at the price of crawling, or of backing down in front of Jesse Schell's bullying arrogance. He wasn't a damn poodle dog, to be brought to heel with a snap of the finger, nor was he going to toss aside his own plans for the future just to suit the whim of others.

There was quality in the Creagers. Ordinarily, old Alec was a scrupulously honest, fair minded man, but he had some of the blind spots of the old line cattleman. Particularly as regarding squatters and any idea of change from the old ways he worshipped. He was strongly jealous of what he regarded as the God-given rights of a cattleman.

And there was no one quite like Joyce. No one with her fine swift grace, the beauty of her dark head, her pride and immaculateness of spirit. But she was blindly devoted to her father, and his opinions were her opinions, completely and without question. And why neither of them could see through the crude, heavy brutishness that lay in Jesse Schell, Larkin could not understand.

He sat his saddle there in the wide still night, Britt Larkin did, thinking on these things until his cigarette was smoked out. Then, in abrupt decision, he pointed his horse's head for town, for Fort Cord.

Fort Cord was a weather-beaten sign post along the trail of empire. Back in the days of the Modoc Indian trouble, it had been a military post and headquarters. With the final subjugation of the Modocs, it had lost its importance, the military moved out and the wide miles of the reservation went back to the frontier.

Britt Larkin rode slowly the length of the single street, wondering where he'd most likely find Len Revis. He knew Len was still in town, else he'd have met him along the trail. Garrulous old Len might still be at the general store, swapping range gossip with Henry Castro, or he might be in the Guidon, sitting into a few hands of low limit stud poker. Larkin decided to try the store first.

He dismounted and tied in front of the place and caught Henry Castro in the act of closing up for the night. Henry Castro was a short, round faced man, blunt and acid in his comment.

"Where you been, that you don't know?" he snapped, in answer to Larkin's question.

Larkin stiffened. "Don't know what?"

"Why, that Obe Widdens and Duke Nulk ganged Len and beat him half to death. Enough to make a dog sick. Len being as old as he is, and the two of them jumping him."

"Where's Len now?" Larkin's question was thin and tight.

"Up at Sam Garfield's hotel. I helped Hack Dinwiddie take Len up there and put him to bed.

Sam's Missis is doctoring Len. Nothin' busted, she says. But Len's got a good week in bed ahead of him."

"When and where did it happen?"

"Over in front of the Guidon," explained Castro. "Jesse Schell and his outfit had just come to town. Len met up with them. I don't know for sure what led to the fracas; musta been words of some kind. Anyhow, I heard a couple of yells and came out on my porch. I could see there was some sort of fight goin' on, but there wasn't much light comin' from the Guidon windows, so I couldn't tell between who.

"Well, pretty soon all the Running S crowd went into the Guidon. I could make out somebody layin' just at the edge of the light. I went over and saw it was Len. Hack Dinwiddie came along and between us we packed Len up to the hotel. At first he was completely out, but by the time we got him on a bunk he'd come back some. We couldn't get much out of him except that Widdens and Nulk ganged him. What you goin' to do about it, Britt?"

"See Len, first."

Sam Garfield's hotel was one wing of what had been the old military barracks, the rest of which had been made into a warehouse and the stage company's headquarters. Larkin met Hack Dinwiddie at the hotel door. Hack was a tremendous man, powerful, but slow and ponderous. Ordinarily the best natured sort, he was now scowling darkly.

"Len?" asked Larkin.

Hack jerked his head. "In there, beginnin' to come out of it. Me, I'm goin' over to the Guidon to have a talk with a couple of scurvy whelps."

"You wait right here, Hack," Larkin said grimly. "As Len's boss, that's my chore. Widdens and Nulk were hitting at me through Len. I'm seeing Len first, then we'll both go over to the Guidon."

Sam and Mrs. Garfield were with Len. He had taken it, all right. His gaunt face was battered and cut and darkly livid with bruises. Both eyes were swelled shut. Mrs. Garfield was applying compresses to bring down the swelling. Larkin leaned over the bed.

"This is Britt, Len. How you feeling?"

Len stirred. "Boy!" he mumbled. His battered lips twisted in what was meant for a smile. "Like I'd been run over by a stage. Might have been able to handle Widdens, but when Nulk pitched in, too — that was rough. Should have kept my big mouth shut, I reckon. Don't fuss about me. I'll be up and around tomorrow."

"You'll be up and around in a week, if you're lucky," said stout, kindly Mrs. Garfield. "Britt, you get out of here. Len needs quiet, not talk."

Larkin gripped one of Len's gaunt paws tightly, then left the room, drawing Sam Garfield with him. "Sam, how did this thing start? Len's no trouble hunter, nor yet a fool."

"I only know what I heard," said Sam. "Seems Jesse Schell and the Running S are all frothed up at you for some reason. When they met up with Len, Widdens started throwing talk against you and Len called him a damn liar. That set it off."

"I see. Thanks, Sam."

As Larkin turned away, Sam caught him by the arm. "Now don't you go get in a mess. You can't tangle with the whole Running S layout. And they're in an ugly temper."

Larkin's answer had a cold ring to it. "I'm in quite a temper myself, Sam."

Hack Dinwiddie was waiting outside, prowling up and down. Hack was strictly a man of peace until anger got the best of him. Now that first hot edge of anger was wearing off and there was a hint of doubt in his voice.

"I've been thinkin', Britt. Mebbe you better not —"

"Never think at a time like this, Hack," Larkin cut in.

He headed for the Guidon, walking fast. Big Hack lumbered along behind him. Running S horses made a dark group along the hitch rail. A smaller group of mounts stood further along, these belonging to the Three Link men whom Alec Creager had allowed to come to town. These things Larkin noted mechanically, shadows along the outer fringes of the purpose which gripped him.

The breath of the saloon was hot and smoky, the bar well filled with Jesse Schell looming big and blonde in the center of things. Nearest the door were the Three Link riders, one of them being their foreman, Tom Adin. He was a spare, angular man, grizzled, his expression just now still and taciturn. Adin turned his head as Larkin and Hack Dinwiddie entered. His eyes flickered and he kept turning until his back was to the bar and his elbows braced against it, and he could watch the room and all that went on in it.

Obe Widdens was a couple of places removed from Jesse Schell, on this side of him. Duke Nulk was about in a similar spot, on the other side. A Running S rider, sighting Larkin, growled a low warning and the whole outfit came around to face the door. Jesse Schell stared a moment, then his heavy lips curled.

"How come, Larkin? Thought you were going to spend the night, makin' up to those squatters?"

Larkin paid Jesse no attention. He moved straight up to Obe Widdens. He saw that Len Revis had got in a few licks, for one corner of Widdens' mouth was swollen and there was a bruise up under his left eye. With two jerks, Larkin unbuckled his gun belt and tossed it on the bar.

"All right, Obe," he said thinly. "Take yours off. I'm going to see just how good you are with somebody nearer your own age. And after you, we'll have a look at Mister Nulk!"

Back along the bar, Tom Adin said, "Ah!" in a soft, curt way, then came pushing swiftly up. "This," he added, "makes sense. All right, Widdens — take your gun off!"

Surprised, Larkin swung his head. "Not your mix, Tom."

"Makin' it so," was the terse answer. "All my life I've loved an even break. Now we'll have one." Then, as Jesse Schell began to elbow out, Tom Adin added with a quick, ringing note, "Jesse, you stay put!"

Now it was Hack Dinwiddie locking a big hand on Jesse's shoulder, pushing him back. "That's the ticket, Tom. Schell stays put!"

The growl that had begun to lift among the Running S crew died out under the cool flash in Tom Adin's eyes. They shuffled restlessly, but that was all.

Obe Widdens, his glance on Larkin, rubbed the palms of his hands across the front of his shirt and started to sidle away from the bar. It was plain that he had no intention of taking off his gun, so Larkin, sliding a quick step forward, hit him a straight lashing smash to the face. It spun Widdens back toward the bar and Tom Adin, moving swiftly, grabbed Obe's gun and jerked it away.

"Now," said Adin calmly, "he's all yours, Britt!"

Larkin went after his man savagely and without mercy. It had been building up in him, since back along the timber road earlier in the night, when Obe had taunted him from the dark.

Hugging his bony head with his arms, crimson already shining down his chin from Larkin's blow, Obe managed to get away from the bar, and with the fury of desperation, uncoiled suddenly and swung at Larkin's head. Larkin took most of the blow on a hunched shoulder, the balance tipping him a little as it landed under his ear. Then he was storming all over Obe, sinking both fists deep into Obe's gaunt midriff.

This brought Obe over, hunched and gasping. Larkin spread his feet and uppercut his man wickedly, feeling Obe's nose crumple under the bite of his knuckles. That did it, as far as Obe Widdens was concerned. He gave back fast, bloody and dazed. But Larkin trapped him against a poker table, clubbed him twice to the side of the head, straightened him with a left, then knocked him half way across the table with a right fist that landed with the sound of a flat board slapped hard against water.

Obe Widdens rolled off the table and stayed on the floor wanting no more of this sort of business. Larkin stood over him, taunting him through tight lips.

"Come on, Obe — get up and take the rest of it! Come on, you saffron gutted whelp! Get up on your feet!"

Obe acted like he didn't hear. He merely propped his elbows on the floor, nursed his battered face in his spread hands, snuffling and bubbling through his broken nose.

Larkin turned away, moved further along the bar, his face bleak and stony. "All right, Nulk. Now it's you!"

Duke Nulk was short and wide and thick,

always smelling of stale sweat. He had more confidence in himself than Obe Widdens did at this sort of game. In fact, he knew a certain brutal pride in his rough and tumble ability. Now, knowing there was no other way out of this affair, he made no attempt at stalling or avoiding the issue. He lowered his head and came at Larkin in a driving rush.

He came in surprisingly fast for one of his squat bulk, and Larkin got only partially clear. He warded off one of Nulk's clubbing fists, but the other thudded home to the side of his head and knocked him spinning to one side.

Jesse Schell, silent up to now, yelled thickly. "Good work, Duke! Now get him!"

Nulk tried. He whirled, dived after Larkin, trapped him against a wall, got both arms about Larkin's middle, butted his bullet head against Larkin's chin, tried to cripple Larkin's feet with hard trampling boot heels.

Larkin knew immediately that here was a far tougher handful than Obe Widdens had been. This fellow Nulk was fast and powerful. There had been plenty of weight behind his first blow and now his butting head was jarring Larkin and starting a trickle of blood across his lips.

Abruptly Nulk lunged upward, driving a bunched knee at Larkin's crotch. And only the fact that Larkin was at the moment twisting his hips in an effort to break clear, saved him from Nulk's attempt to cripple. And now, where Larkin had merely known cold purpose against

Obe Widdens, a sudden black fury convulsed him.

He brought both hands up inside, clamped them on either side of Nulk's heavy jaw, then drove upward with every ounce of strength he knew. For a moment or two Nulk resisted the lift, but even the power in his thick bull neck was not enough to hold against this pressure. His head snapped back, a strangled grunt broke from him and he fell away from Larkin, beating the air with his arms, trying to regain his balance.

For the moment he was wide open, and Larkin threw the hardest punch of his life. It caught Nulk full in the center of the face and Nulk teetered and reeled, his eyes going blank and stupid. He did not go down, but his arms fell loose by his sides and his head rolled.

Larkin hit him again, the same way and in the same place. Nulk slammed back against the bar, bounced off and ran into a third devastating smash. Nulk dropped to his knees, bowed slowly forward until his head touched the floor, then fell over on his side.

On spread feet, Larkin weaved from side to side, close to going down himself. For in that last bursting surge to break clear and then drive home those three murderous punches, it seemed that everything had drained out of him. There was blood across his lips and raw strain dragging through his chest. His words came hoarsely as he wheeled slowly to face Jesse Schell.

"Should have been you — taking that, Jesse.

They're — your dogs. You probably — sicced them on — old Len. Yeah — that should have been — for you . . . !"

Jesse Schell, exultant one moment when he saw Duke Nulk gain first advantage over Larkin, but now swollen with temper at sight of both Nulk and Widdens stupid and helpless on the floor, made as if to lunge for Larkin. But Tom Adin's hooking elbow drove him back.

"No go, Jesse! Not now. Britt's done enough for one night. You'd like him the way he is now, wouldn't you — just about wore down? There's times, Jesse, when you're awful hard to stomach!"

There was a cold, biting contempt in Tom Adin's words. Now, in milder tone, he turned to Hack Dinwiddie. "Hack, you get Larkin out of here."

Hack took Larkin's gun off the bar and then, with the broad power of his chest, herded Larkin out into the night. "For your own good, boy — for your own good," he rumbled.

At first Larkin tried to resist. Then, as the anger burned less hotly in him, he went along, grateful for Hack's support. The night air helped, running cool and sweet into his laboring lungs. Presently they were at Hack's own cabin, out back of the blacksmith shop. Larkin eased down on the bunk while Hack fumbled around and got a lamp going.

There was still some warm water in the kettle and Hack poured this into a basin. "Dive into that," he ordered. "Do you good."

Larkin went over to the bench and washed up, strength and coordination coming back to him. He was deep in the folds of a towel when the door opened and Tom Adin came in, carrying Larkin's hat. He looked at Larkin with just a hint of a twinkle.

"Thought you'd probably need this. It's still a pretty good hat. And," he added, "it seems to belong to a pretty good man."

Larkin looked at him between dabs with the towel. "Obliged, Tom. But I don't quite understand. Right now I'm the most unpopular cattleman in these parts — with other cattlemen."

Tom Adin laid the hat on the cabin table, built a cigarette. His face was still and taciturn again. He inhaled deeply and turned to leave, pausing a moment in the cabin door.

"I always liked Len Revis," he said. "Tonight, I like you."

Then he was gone, the door closing behind him.

"Tom's deep, and nobody's fool," rumbled Hack Dinwiddie. "Besides being a square, up and down hombre. Well, how you feeling now?"

Larkin managed a flickering grin. "Think I'll live. But I'll have a few spots in the morning to remind me. If I hadn't managed to break loose from Nulk, he'd have butted my brains out. Tough bucko, that feller."

"Damned animal!" snorted Hack. "Hey, you're not going trouble hunting again, are you?

You better stay right here for the night. You can use my spare bunk."

Larkin had picked up his hat and donned it. Now he was buckling on his gun. "Got things to do, bright and early tomorrow morning, Hack. Did Len tell you about coming out and shoeing the cavvy string?"

Hack nodded. "When he first hit town tonight. I'll be there."

"Fine! Obliged, big feller, for everything. Be seeing you."

Going over to get his horse from the rail in front of Henry Castro's store, Larkin looked up street and saw that the Running S saddle broncs still stood in front of the Guidon. Evidently he'd wrung more water out of Obe Widdens and Duke Nulk than he thought.

Larkin let his horse set its own pace. At this hour, night had its full grip on the world, the moist cool pressure of it bleeding the aromatic pungency from the sage and laying it thick and invisible, almost a flavor across a man's tongue.

Out ahead the Royales pushed blackly up against the chilling stars and sent down a breath of night wind to play across the sage. From the first elevation of the foothills, Larkin looked down across the river flats and saw that all was darkness there. The squatter camp was settled for the night.

He was well up into the chill, black shadow of the timber when he caught the first mutter of hoofs coming up behind him and he knew it was the Running S. But the Running S turn-off was close at hand and he was well past this when Schell and his outfit took it and the sound of their progress grew muffled and faded out to the north west. As usual, they were pushing their horses. That, reflected Larkin, was Jesse Schell's way. He had no mercy on either man or beast.

Chapter III

PROMISE OF THE EARTH

AT MID-MORNING the following day, Britt Larkin rode in on the squatter camp for the second time in twenty-four hours. Aside from a swollen lip and a dark bruise on the left side of his face, he looked his usual self. But he was stiff and sore from head to toe, and he held his horse to its easiest riding gait.

The squatter wagons still stood as they had the night before; they seemed to be resting up for a future still in doubt. Either that or they were being kept bunched in case of attack by cattle interests still hostile. Larkin inquired for Cass Partee and was directed, civilly enough, further along the flat. He found Partee helping Oake Calloway cold shoe a team of horses.

A tub of laundry was boiling and steaming over a nearby fire, tended by Rose Calloway. She straightened as Larkin rode up, brushed a wisp of hair back from her face and smiled. She was pretty, all right, with a grave, steady sweetness in her eyes and about her mouth. Larkin touched his hat to her and walked over to Cass Partee, who looked at him keenly.

"I hope your trouble didn't come because of us, Larkin."

"Trouble? Oh, this?" Larkin touched his bruised face, shrugged. "Not at all. This was over something that's been stewing in the pot for a long time."

Oake Calloway, squatted down, a hoof of one of the team hooked over a knee, made a couple more passes with his rasp, dropped the hoof and came erect.

"From what I've seen over the space of a damn few hours," he said shrewdly, "I'd say it would be mighty difficult for any self-respecting man to live in these parts very long without coming to trouble with that Schell hombre. There's one feller who sure pushes the fur of the cat the wrong way."

"Jesse can be quite a problem, for a fact," admitted Larkin. "When you men finish with that shoeing chore, I got a proposition to talk over with you. No rush, though."

He dropped on his heels and rolled a cigarette. He knew that all around him a number of people were watching him, weighing him, guessing at his intent. He saw grim, truculent old Sod Tremper stalk stiffly by and the old squatter's eyes burned with dislike and suspicion, and Larkin knew that Tremper still questioned his friendliness.

You couldn't, mused Larkin, blame these

people for their attitude. It was the product of years of pushing around, of hostility toward them all across the cattle country. They were what they were because they owned a tough, ingrained love of the earth and of the things they could grow out of it.

Where a cowman measured his life in terms of open range with cattle grazing on it, these folk thought in terms of the plow and of crops lifting to the benevolent sun. In a country of their own kind they were lords of the earth. In country like this they were outcasts, harried and hated. And they could not be blamed if they answered suspicion and animosity with like currency. Larkin wondered if what he had in mind to propose to them would have any effect.

Not all of the folk were too critical of him. A small, tow headed girl of six or seven came sidling up, watching Larkin with bright, round, childish eyes. Her hair was braided into pig tails so tight they stuck out from her head like prongs. Larkin grinned at her and she was all confusion, eyes downcast, digging her bare brown toes into the ground and wriggling like an ingratiating puppy. Larkin made a mental note that the next time he was in town, he'd raid Henry Castro's candy case.

And then there was Rose Calloway, busy yonder at her laundry tub. Her smile of welcome was open, genuine and sincere. No man, thought Larkin, could look at that girl and not admire her. Her natural vigor and grace, the tawny mass of her hair, the firm, clean brownness of her. He found himself comparing her with Joyce Creager, and though he knew a slight sense of guilt about it, he had to admit that she did not suffer from it.

Within the next half hour, Cass Partee and Oake Calloway finished their horse shoeing job and they came over to Larkin, scrubbing sweat from their faces. "We're ready to listen," said Calloway.

Larkin got to his feet. "Let's take a little walk."

He led them away from camp and out into the tall, thick sage. There he stopped and swung an encompassing arm.

"We're standing on some mighty good soil. The size and thickness of this sage proves it. If a man was to clear this land and put water on it, he could grow anything."

Oake Calloway nodded. "Agree with you. But clearing this land stacks up as considerable of a chore, and as for water, where would it come from? The river bed's lower than where we stand, and I never yet saw water that would run up hill."

"True enough," said Larkin. "But cast your eyes up yonder." He pointed again, to the east, where Reservation Valley narrowed and lost itself in a tangle of low, looping hills. "Back there the Saber River breaks past a spine of rock near the mouth of a gorge, a gorge you can easily toss a rock across. Where it comes out of the gorge the river jumps off a falls maybe fifty or sixty feet high. In the old days the Indians called the falls White Thunder. From the crest of the falls down to these flats is a steady, even slope. It wouldn't take much of a dam at the right spot in the gorge to put a steady head of water in an irrigation ditch that would bring the water to this spot we stand on."

Oake Calloway stared into the distance with narrowed eyes. "It's a chore that gets bigger by the minute," he said drily. "There'd be a hell of a lot of ditch to be dug. Which would take money and labor — a lot of both."

"Not so much as you might think," Larkin said. "Oh, I'm not saying it would be easy, understand. But I've checked this proposition a dozen times. There's a gulch — you can't see it from here — and it works along the north slope of the valley and heads up blind not over a hundred feet from the mouth of the gorge. A ten foot dam up there, and a cut through to the head of the gulch, and that gulch would deliver water to within a mile and a half of the flats. That would be the amount of ditch to be dug — a mile and a half."

Oake Calloway still had that far away look in his eyes. He got out a blackened old briar pipe, loaded and lighted it, tamped down the glowing tobacco with the tip of a horny forefinger. Then he turned abruptly and looked at Larkin with grim intensity.

"Personally, I've come to like the look of you, Larkin. I believe you mean well by us people.

But I got a pretty fair workin' knowledge of human nature, and that just won't let me believe that yo're pointin' out all this to Cass and me just out of the goodness of your heart. You got a stake in this somewhere and you figure to benefit by it. Am I right?"

"Dead right," admitted Larkin frankly. "I was coming to that angle. Up yonder in the high parks of the Royales I got quite a sizable herd of cattle. Alec Creager's got more than I have — a lot more. Jesse Schell's got his share. Then there's half a dozen smaller outfits that graze further back in the Royales than we do. It all sums up, come shipping season, to a lot of cattle coming out of the Royales and across country to the shipping pens on the railroad at Button Willow."

Larkin paused and spun another smoke, conscious of the close attention Calloway and Cass Partee were paying to his words.

"Most of the cattle, when they come out of the mountains, are fat and in good shape," he went on. "But while there are watering stops along the drive trail to Button Willow, there's damn little graze. So the cattle shed fat, and fast, on the drive. And that fat is money, lost to the owner. I've seen a critter lose damn near half its value on the drive between here and Button Willow. And that just don't make sense to me, when something can be done to change it."

Oake Calloway nodded slowly. "I'm not a cattleman, but I can sure see your point. How can the present setup be changed?"

"Like this. It's an idea I've had for a long time, but I never saw any chance of putting it to work until you people showed up here and set up camp. First, it means sage cleared off this land. Second, it means water on the land, with people down here growing crops, grain and corn and hay. Then it means a deal between those people and us cattlemen, which will put feed corrals on the flats, and feed stations set up at the water stops all along the way between here and Button Willow, so that when we put a critter on the cars at Button Willow it'll have a full belly and some fat on its ribs. It could mean a deal between the cattlemen and the people on these flats that will make money for both."

Cass Partee, who had been listening intently, nodded vehemently. "Larkin, you make me see things."

Oake Calloway, puffing slowly, bobbed his head up and down. "I can see some of that myself. But," he reminded, "so far there's just one of these cattlemen you mention who can look at us and not curse us. That one is you. We'd need others, to make this thing pay."

"A cattleman," said Larkin, "thinks in terms of cattle, feed and water. He'll not fight and destroy anything which will provide either the feed or the water. Not if he's any kind of a man at all, and most of them are. The big trouble has been that for too long cattlemen have thought of the squatter in terms of a tar paper shanty and a line of barb wire fence cutting his cattle off from a water hole or a stretch of range grass. But here's a whole river of water, and no grass — just useless sage brush so damned thick grass can't grow. Show him in concrete terms where you can benefit him and you'll end up making him a friend."

"That fellow Schell," growled Calloway, "could never be a friend of mine."

"Forget Schell," said Larkin. "Alec Creager is the big cattle influence in the Royales. Whichever way Creager goes, that's the way it will be."

Again Oake Calloway stared into the distance, weighing the past, the present and the future. He sighed deeply. "You tempt me, Larkin. I been driftin' a long time. Not because I wanted to, but because I had to. There's a lot of others like me. Mebbe a lot of it is our own fault. We scare too easy. And there's a reason for that, too. This is the first time I ever saw a gatherin' of my kind in one place, big enough to really make a fight of it if we have to. Most generally it's been two or three families. That ain't enough to stand much pressure. But right here in these flats we got nigh on to twenty able-bodied men. If they'll all stick, we could make a stand of it, all right."

Calloway was silent again. Then his voice came as little more than a murmur, with a note of yearning in it. "We could have fields, real fields, not some dinky little acre of hard scrabble. We could set our roots deep, and grow."

"All of that," prompted Larkin quietly. "And real homes for your women folks, and a school for the kids. You'd be set, Mr. Calloway."

"It would take money and tools," Calloway said. "We could supply the labor, but there is little money among us."

"Let me worry about the money and tools," said Larkin. "Your job is to sell the plan to your friends. Spread yourself, talk it straight. Make them see what I think I've made you see. The plan is sound. It can be done."

A glow had come into Oake Calloway's eyes. He was a man seeing opportunity. The more he thought of it, the bigger and finer it became. "I'll talk," he promised. "I can't promise the result, but I can promise the talk. I'll do my damndest, Larkin!"

"And here," spoke up Cass Partee. "Some we'll convince, some we'll shame. And Rose, she'll talk to the women, make them see those homes, and that school."

"That's the stuff!" applauded Larkin. "I'll drop by again in a day or two and see what the final answer is."

They shook hands on it.

A little over an hour later, Larkin rode into Fort Cord. His first stop was at the hotel and he went in to see how Len Revis was making out. Len's face looked considerably better through the ministrations of Mrs. Garfield. And Len was willing to admit he'd been considerably optimistic about being up and around in a day.

"That Duke Nulk!" he mumbled. "He's worse'n a bear. When he hits you he hurts you plumb to your heels. Think I mighta done a pretty fair job of keepin' the flies off Obe Widdens if Nulk had stayed out of it. But I heard how you curried them two jingos, boy. That was a fool thing to do, take 'em both on one after the other, just on my account."

Larkin grinned down at the old rider. "I suppose you went after Widdens just because you didn't like the shape of his head? If sticking up for a friend makes a fool of a man, then there's a pair of us who qualify. Now don't you try and rush things, fellah. Don't you head for the ranch until you're really up to it. Me and the Dodd boys can take care of things."

Leaving the hotel, Larkin heard the clangor of hammer on anvil beating out a melody in the still, warm air. Which meant Hack Dinwiddie was at work in his blacksmith shop. Larkin drifted over there and found Hack bent over, fitting a shoe to the front of a racy looking sorrel. And on an empty nail keg, Joyce Creager sat, watching Hack at work.

She stirred slightly at sight of Larkin and gave only a brief nod in response to his quiet, "Hello, Joyce."

Hack dropped the sorrel's hoof, stepped over and plunged the hot shoe into the water tub, where it hissed and sizzled. He looked up at Larkin. "How you feelin'?"

Larkin smiled. "I can find some sore spots

without looking too far. Just saw Len. He's coming along. When do you figure you can come out to the ranch and do that cavvy job?"

"Headin' out later this afternoon. Had a couple of jobs to clean up first. You must be figgerin' on a lot of ridin' in the near future?"

"Quite a bit. See you later, Hack."

Hack said, "While you're ridin', don't spend all your time lookin' at stars, boy. After you left last night I went back to the Guidon. Jesse Schell was still tryin' to get Widdens and Nulk straightened out. You really put some kinks in that pair." Hack withdrew the shoe from the cooling tub, put it in his vise and began to rasp the scale off it. "You keep off the top of ridges, Britt."

Larkin, watching Joyce Creager from the corner of his eye, saw her stir again at Hack's warning words. He said, "They're surly dogs, Hack. They won't bite while you're lookin' at them."

"That's just my point," averred Hack. "Yes, sir, just my point."

From the blacksmith shop, Larkin went over to Henry Castro's store. Castro was alone, slouched in a round backed chair, reading a tattered newspaper. He looked at Larkin over the top of his steel-rimmed spectacles.

"You must be pretty whangy. Up and around and cricket spry after that ruckus last night."

"Things to do, Henry," said Larkin. "How much is my credit good for, and for how long?"

Castro folded the newspaper and dropped it

beside his chair. "Depends. How much you want and what for?"

"Well, let's start off with quite a lot of giant powder, along with fuse and caps. There'll be sledge hammers and rock drills. There'll be picks and shovels, a couple of dozen each. And say three hundred feet of good heavy chain in various lengths. Outside of that, all I'll want are two or three Fresno scrapers, lumber, nails and a flock of other odds and ends I can't think of just now."

"Humph!" growled Castro. "Why stop there? Why don't you ask for my right arm, my shirt and pants and mebbe my back teeth? Just what kind of a locoed idea are you playin' with?

"I ain't agreein' to a thing, understand," stated Castro. "But I'll listen — and keep my mouth shut."

Larkin perched on the counter, built a cigarette and began to talk. He laid the whole plan in front of the storekeeper and, as he got deeper into it, slid off the counter and paced up and down. Henry Castro sat utterly still, hands folded across his little fat stomach. When Larkin finished, Castro mused for a time in thoughtful silence. Then he stirred.

"One weak spot, Britt. The squatters. They won't stick. Time Jesse Schell and Alec Creager get through pushing them around, those squatters will flit. And then where'd you be, boy? You couldn't afford to bring in a laboring gang to finish up the job. And even if you could, there'd be all those crops to be planted and tended and harvested. To make the idea go, you got to have the squatters. And I tell you, they won't stick."

"I'm hoping to swing Alec Creager behind the plan before I get done with him," said Larkin. "Alec's no fool. He's stubborn and hard to handle in some ways, but he's a fair man, and once he really sees the benefits the plan can bring him, I'm sure he'll come around. For he's sound-headed where a dollar is concerned."

"Maybe," conceded Castro. "But you'll never bring Jesse Schell around; he'll buck you every foot of the way. He'll rip and tear, Jesse will."

"I expect that," nodded Larkin, a toughening note coming into his tone. "But Jesse will get more than he sends. I'm getting kinda tired of Jesse. It's high time this country slapped him down."

"Agree with you there. But he'll take considerable slapping before he'll stay down. And he's got a regular hex, or something, where a squatter is concerned. He'll never lay off 'em. And the squatters won't stand the pressure. I know the breed. They'll pull out and leave you flat."

"Not this bunch, Henry. There's some pretty stout folks among 'em. I've already given them some hint of what the deal could mean to them, and they like the picture." Larkin took another turn up and down the store, before coming to a stop in front of Castro. Abruptly his face was stone bleak and his eyes cold. "I believe in my plan, Henry — believe in it all the way. And before I'll stand for Jesse Schell spoiling it with his damn blind stupidity, I'll kill him!"

Henry Castro stared. "Why, you mean that, don't you?"

"Yes," said Larkin steadily. "I mean it!"

The storekeeper went silent for a time, polishing his spectacles with a corner of a faded bandana handkerchief. "I like the picture you paint, Britt," he admitted finally. "I like it a lot. It would be a great thing for this valley, if you could put it across. It's sound, it makes sense. If I could only feel that the squatters would stick!"

"Somehow I feel that they will, Henry. I feel it enough that I'm going to stake everything I have in the world on that belief. That's how sure I am."

Castro got up, went to the door of the store, stared out at the street, hands shoved into his hip pockets. Abruptly he whirled.

"Tell you what, Britt. You get even a half way nod from Alec Creager, I'll throw in with you. For I'm tired of seein' nothing but empty sage brush in Reservation Valley, and good land going to waste. Damn it, I'll go even further. If you can get nothing more out of Creager than just a promise that he won't interfere, I'll go you. What if I do lose my shirt? I've already spent too much of my life, mousing around this damn store. I'd sure like to feel that I had some kind of hand in doing something really big, before I die. Yeah, you get Alec Creager to agree not to interfere, and I'll go you. Of course, I ain't got any small part of what you want in stock, but I can get it from Johnson & Page, in Button Willow. When you going to see Creager?"

"Right away. Today."

Hoofs thudded softly to a stop in front of the store, then quick, light steps crossed the porch. Joyce Creager came in.

"Any mail for Three Link, Mr. Castro?" she asked.

"Some, as I recollect, Joyce." Castro went over behind the counter to the mail rack and began shuffling through a handful of envelopes and other matter.

The girl paid Larkin no attention and he went out quietly, thinking that Joyce Creager would always bring the fine, clean breath of the outdoors into any room she entered. He got his horse and was waiting at the edge of town when she came riding out on her way home. He swung his mount in beside her spirited sorrel.

"We're heading the same way, Joyce," he said.

"The trail," she said stiffly, "is free. But maybe I prefer to ride it alone."

She would have lifted the sorrel to a run, but Larkin leaned over and caught her rein and, when she turned on him angrily, met her look calmly.

"I'm riding all the way to Three Link with you, Joyce. I want to see your father about something. Let's be neighborly about this."

He watched the anger flood her face and throat, watched until her glance slid away in some confusion. Then he let go of her rein and straightened in his saddle. "That's better."

She held the sorrel to a jog, but she wouldn't look at Larkin, keeping her head swung the other way, her head and shoulders uncompromisingly stiff. They covered a full two miles in complete silence. Then Larkin, having spun up a cigarette, spoke almost casually through the smoke.

"I don't understand it. I really don't, Joyce. A few weeks ago you wouldn't have objected at all to my riding home with you. In fact, I like to believe you might have even welcomed me along. Why all this sudden change? I'm exactly the same man now that I was then. Oh, I admit I don't see eye to eye with your father on the squatter question, or maybe on the quality of beef cattle. But if you give me time, maybe he and I will see things a little more evenly. In the meantime, can't you and me be friends? We used to be. Pretty good friends, too."

Color swept up her throat again and now, for the first time since leaving town, she met his glance fully.

"Some things," she said stiffly, "are unforgivable in a man. One is, that he be a traitor to his own kind."

"And you really think I am such?"

"After last night, what else could I believe?" she flared. "You were with the squatters. You took their part. You stood up for them. And before that you refused to add your name to the warnings Dad and Jesse Schell posted. That —"

"Would do no good and I knew it," cut in Larkin. "I was proven right, wasn't I? The squatters are here. For that matter, neither Alec nor I, nor Jesse Schell or anybody else had any right to post warning signs. For none of us own this valley land. It's open land, Government land, free to any man who wants to set up a homestead here according to the law. If the squatters intend to do such, who are we to say they can't?"

The deepening color in her cheeks betrayed the rising feeling in her. "Only a fool welcomes squatters into cattle country."

Behind this girl, thought Larkin bleakly, he could hear Alec Creager clearly speaking. Her words were exactly as Creager would have given them.

"This I read in a book one time," said Larkin. "Once there was a king, a king named Canute. He had the idea he was so great and his power so much, he could go down to the edge of the sea and order the tide not to come in. He got his feet wet. In a way, Joyce, people are a tide, flowing over the land. And I don't figure myself any king, trying to stop the unstoppable. Does that make me a fool?"

It wasn't her good sense answering, but instead the thoughtless retort of a young, somewhat uncertain person parroting the words and thoughts of a father whom she worshipped blindly. This, and the desire to hit out when being argued into a corner.

"Yes," she burst forth. "A fool, and a weak

one! For only such a fool would turn against his own kind and throw away their respect and regard for the sake of a colony of shiftless, worthless squatters!"

Britt Larkin reached over, caught her rein again, brought both horses to a stop. He was making all the allowances he could for Joyce Creager. He knew the dominance her father held over her beliefs and feelings. But Joyce was no longer a child. She was a young woman, and a lovely one, and old enough to think for herself.

If she hadn't been who she was, her remarks would have meant little. But when a man had thought as much of a girl as he had of Joyce Creager, then the lash of bitter words could bite deep. Larkin looked at her with narrowed eyes and a bite of harshness came into his voice.

"Fair enough. You've just voiced an opinion, which I guess is your right. Now it's my turn. You were beautiful the first time I ever saw you, Joyce. No, I think lovely is a better word. You are still lovely, even more than ever. But you're a spoiled baby, the spoiled baby of a domineering father, and a rich, powerful outfit. You never had to do a lick of work you didn't want to do."

He saw her catch her breath, saw the rising flame of anger in her cheeks. But he went on remorselessly.

"Always you've had comfort and security. Four stout walls around you and a tight roof over your head. You've never known want or hardship or worry over the future. You've been petted and pampered and admired. You've let your father do all your thinking for you, and you've never been interested in anyone but yourself long enough to understand that other people in the world have a few rights. And it's a pity such things are so, for you are — very lovely."

Her face had gone crimson, then white, then crimson again. She struggled for words, finally found them.

"Let go of my rein! Let go — !"

And when Larkin made no move to obey, she caught at her quirt, her eyes blazing. She aimed a slashing blow at his face. He put up his free hand, caught the quirt, jerked it from her hand. The pull of this brought her leaning in her saddle, almost over against him, her face but inches from his own. And Larkin, tipping his head, kissed her full on her furious lips.

Larkin laughed with little mirth. "Lovely," he said. "But empty."

He let go of her rein and the sorrel started to run. But the girl set the animal back, rearing and whirling. She scrubbed her lips with the back of a gauntleted hand.

"You'll pay for that," she raged. "You'll pay — !"

Larkin nodded. "Yes, I probably will. Because I'll remember it all my life."

"Dad," she choked. "Jesse Schell. They'll — they'll — !"

"We'll see about Jesse," cut in Larkin. "Here he comes, now!"

Chapter IV

DARK TIDES

JESSE SCHELL was alone, a heavy figure above the sage until the trail made its sharp turn and brought him straight toward them. Because of the distance and the shifting dust, he hadn't actually seen the brief moment of struggle when Larkin had pulled Joyce Creager to him and kissed her. But as he came up he could not mistake the white rage of the girl, nor the grim recklessness of Larkin's faint smile, and so read the tension which lay between them. He swung his heavy glance from one to the other.

"What goes on here?" he demanded. "What's the matter, Joyce?"

Larkin waited, watching the girl. He saw her fight to get a grip on herself, her head lifting proudly.

"Nothing," she said. "Nothing at all, Jesse. We — just had a few words."

Schell grunted skeptically. "You're mad. Something set you off. What was it?"

She bit her lips, shook her head. "Nothing," she said again.

Larkin caught her searing glance, then touched the brim of his hat, almost like a salute. He leaned far over in his saddle, caught up her quirt off the ground and handed it to her.

Jesse Schell swung his glance back and forth, uncertainty and jealous temper in his expression. He shot his next question at Larkin.

"That quirt — did Joyce go to use it on you?"

"Did she?" murmured Larkin.

"If I thought you'd given her just cause, I'd — !"

"You'd what?"

Jesse ground his teeth. "I'd rid this range forever of a damn mealy-mouthed, slickery, squatter-loving — !"

"Shut up, Jesse!"

Larkin's words hit with a crackle. He moved his horse forward until its chest was almost jammed against the shoulder of Schell's mount. No trace of a smile was on Larkin's face now. Instead, there was a harshness which made his features craggy, and his eyes were charged with a dark, cold intensity. The same chill quality was in his voice.

"There had to come a time for this. It's now. Get off the trail, Jesse!"

Joyce Creager, still seething with emotional tumult, hesitating between the impulse to race away, and a burning pride which would not let her, went still in her saddle, chilled by an ominous something which suddenly charged the air.

The angry color drained from her face and her eyes grew big as she watched these two men.

Jesse Schell, massive and blonde, with his heavy shoulders and heavy features, his face that reddened under the sun, but never browned, dominant and arrogant in all his words and actions. And Britt Larkin, leaner, rangier, sun blackened; features cleanly and now, harshly cut. A man who in the past had smiled easily and seemed to carry life on his shoulders with a sort of easy insouciance. But not now, definitely not now. Against the smooth, hard brownness of his face, his eyes were pits of gray, electric chill.

Larkin said it again. "Get off the trail, Jesse!"

Schell swayed his heavy shoulders forward. "Get off — hell! Who do you think you're talkin' to? I'll run you out of the country. I'll — !"

Larkin pushed his horse a little closer.

"I've listened to that kind of talk long enough, Jesse. Too long. You've spread yourself all over this range, roaring and bellowing, threatening this and that to men if they didn't bow the head or bend the knee. You've pushed and shoved and elbowed, and to hell with the other fellow. You've got yourself to believing you're big as a mountain and twice as tough. But you're not, Jesse, you're not. And I'm going to prove it! You haven't got Obe Widdens or Duke Nulk or anyone else to back your hand now, Jesse. It's just you and me. And you're going to get off the trail!"

Larkin spurred his mount, driving it lunging into Schell's mount, forcing that badgered animal to swing away. Schell brought it back and around with cruel, hard strength. But there was Larkin's horse, rearing a little now, but lunging in again, and there was Larkin, watching with a cold alertness, ready for anything. Once more came the inexorable words.

"Get off the trail, Jesse!"

Now at last did Jesse Schell fully understand. Just the two of them, out here in the lonely sage, all pretense thrown aside, the issue plain and stark. Here was the unspoken issue that had always been there between them, but now for the first time brought really and fully into the open. This was showdown!

Britt Larkin kept forcing his horse in and Jesse Schell's mount was giving way. It was symbolic, this forcing a man off the trail. It was settling something, establishing who was the better man.

Realization of the issue unlocked the well of blind fury that was always couched in Jesse Schell. His florid face suffused and his neck swelled.

"You crazy fool!" he yelled. "You think you can do this to me?"

"You've been making your big talk for a long time," said Larkin. "Now it's my turn and I'm telling you. Get off the trail!"

He sent his horse ahead with another hard lunge and Jesse's horse, whirling at the moment, brought them up flank to flank. Jesse, standing in his stirrups, swung a clubbing fist at Larkin's head. Larkin ducked and the blow landed at the base of his neck. It drove him forward and down and as he fell he grabbed at Schell's thick torso. His hands locked in Schell's belt and Jesse, a little off balance from the effort behind his blow, couldn't resist the drag of Larkin's weight. He toppled in his saddle, grabbed for the horn, missed, and followed Larkin to the ground.

The two horses, riderless now, swung apart, Jesse's lunging a few yards into the sage beyond the trail, Larkin's mount starting back along the trail toward town, but soon answered to long training and stopped over dragging reins.

Back there in the trail, two men were getting to their feet. The impact of the fall had broken Larkin's grip and it had jarred a grunt of breath out of Jesse Schell. For a moment they were content to stand and measure each other. Then, as though by some unspoken signal, they lunged to meet each other.

Both men carried guns, but neither seemed to think of them. This was something that went deeper than the mere matching of gunfire. For a gun, deadly though it might be, was an impersonal thing. Here was a need to come to grips, to pound and beat and maul; to drive battering fists into a hated face, to smash and destroy with bare hands. It was a savage fire, bursting and consuming, that could be slaked in no other way.

For a short space they stood toe to toe, fists driving, Schell swinging, like trying to club something down, while Larkin hit shorter, straighter blows. Both dealt out punishment, both took it, and when they finally broke apart again, Larkin, though showing no visible marks, was shaking a numbed head. As for Jesse Schell, his heavy lips were swollen in a pout and a thin trickle of crimson was beginning to seep across his chin.

Jesse spread his feet, charged in again, mauling, bruising, powerful. His rush carried Larkin off the trail, into the sage, and there they fought and floundered, while the disturbed sage whipped and swayed. Jesse swung a fist that missed, but his forearm, massive as a club, hammered Larkin across the side of the neck, sweeping him off his feet. Half stunned, Larkin landed face down in a clump of sage.

A sound erupted from Jesse's throat, part feral growl, part eager whine. He lunged forward, a bear of a man going in for the kill. But the sage was there and in his headlong, blind rush to get at Larkin, the sage clawed at Jesse's feet, tripping him, bringing him to his knees. From this position Jesse tried to throw himself on Larkin, but Larkin was rolling away, and he was on his feet before Jesse was. And then, as Jesse pushed himself erect once more, Larkin threw a desperate, deadly fist.

It landed full and fair under Jessie's left eye and it split the flesh to the bone. It did more. The impact of it beat past the heavy bone and dazed Jesse. His jaw dropped and he staggered. It was Larkin's turn to move in and follow up an advantage and when he did he ran into a blow that put him wavering on his heels. Now his mouth was seeping crimson.

They glared at each other, half crouched and wickedly intent. They circled, and this movement brought them out into the clear of the trail again. In his rolling tumble in the sage, Larkin had lost his gun, but Jesse still had his, swinging at his hip. But there was no thought of guns in the mind of either of them, yet.

Further along the trail, Joyce Creager was fighting her sorrel to keep it under control, for the spirited animal was spooking and rearing, infected in some strange way by the explosive violence of this thing. Joyce's face was white, her eyes wide with a mixture of fear, revulsion and a fascination she could neither fathom nor resist.

These two bloody, panting men! Britt Larkin silent, Jesse Schell making strange, unintelligible sounds in his thick throat. She saw their first meeting in the trail, saw them lunge into the sage, heard the smash of fists on flesh. And now they were back in the trail again.

Now they came together again, and Joyce Creager saw Larkin's lean body arch like a piece of tempered steel spring, to meet and hold against Schell's superior weight and bulk. Then Larkin spun and broke clear and as Schell, carried forward by his own lunge, drove past, Larkin drove a flashing fist under the big man's ear.

The blow tipped Jesse and he stumbled into the sage again. But he came quickly out again, and Joyce Creager thought of a wounded and enraged bear.

Larkin was waiting for Jesse this time. Some of the numbing effects of those two clubbing blows he'd taken was wearing off. Jesse, his arms hooked and dangling, fists opening and closing like hungry claws, was wide open, so intent was he on coming to close grips again. And Larkin stepped between those reaching paws and hammered Jesse full on the angle of his heavy jaw.

That one dropped Jesse, dropped him in a hulking, floundering heap. It did more than put Jesse down. It awakened in his shocked, foggy mind the realization for the first time that this thing might actually go against him; that despite his bulk and massive strength, this lean, deadly hitting enemy in front of him might emerge victor. With that realization cunning awakened.

Jesse rocked upward, made as though to get to his feet. Instead, throwing himself forward, he grabbed at Larkin's legs. Larkin dropped forward, driving his bunched knees into Jesse's unprotected face. The impact broke Jesse's half formed grip and Larkin rolled free and came to his feet again.

Jesse came up, too, nose pulped, face blood-smeared and wild. The feral growl in his throat became a bawl of berserk frustration. Cunning left him, clear thought of any kind left him. Left only was insensate fury and blind purpose. Head down, shoulders hunched, he came plunging in. And Larkin, knowing that his one hope of survival in this affair was to keep clear of Jesse's full grip, side-stepped the rush and let Jesse flounder by. But he followed his man and was waiting when Jesse turned. Then he hit, twice, winging blows that had everything he owned behind them. Jesse's head rocked, but he didn't go down.

Larkin, having lived all his life in a rugged land among rugged men, had known a few savage and brutal fights before. But he had never met up with anything like this before. Hitting Jesse Schell was like hitting some insensate animal. And when, in return, Jesse landed even a glancing blow, it left numbing agony behind. This fellow Jesse Schell had the power to hurt you, just by laying a clawing hand on you.

Larkin slid out of the way of another rush, hammered Jesse on the temple as he went by. The punch, plus the impetus of the charge, spun Jesse into the sage again, where he tripped and half fell across a clump of the stuff. Yet he came up and around once more, though with just a hint of slowing reflexes.

For a moment he stood, weaving a little. His blonde hair had fallen awry over his forehead, and from under it his eyes glared redly. His mouth sagged open and over his battered lower lip, a mixture of blood and saliva ran. His breath was a panting hoarseness. This furnished a clue which guided Britt Larkin's next move.

He started in, then as quickly ducked back, and Jesse's pawing blow hit nothing. Before

Jesse could recover, Larkin was inside, his head jammed under Jesse's chin, both fists pumping into the thick body in front of him. Two, three — four times he hit, feet spread and set, each blow a lifting effort that came clear up from his solidly set heels.

They wrung gasping grunts from Jesse, each blow did, but he held his ground, pounding fists and forearms across Larkin's back and kidneys.

Desperation gripped Larkin. What was he made of, this burly brute in front of him? How could he reach the fellow's last pit of resistance? Already Larkin's fists were numb from impact, his arms and shoulders aching from the furious power he'd put into his blows. This couldn't go on much longer, or he'd go down himself from pure exhaustion. He dug into his fast draining reservoir of strength and drove home two more lifting punches, bringing them up a little higher, sinking them in under Jesse's heart.

These did it! Jesse gave back, groaning, his heavy legs beginning to bend. Larkin set his teeth, hit him again in the same place and then, as Jesse began to slip downward, hit him twice more on his sagging jaw.

Jesse sagged to his knees, head rolling, big body weaving back and forth. For a moment, despite his hatred of the man, Britt Larkin knew a glimmering of respect. For he'd always felt that behind Jesse Schell's heavy arrogance, behind his loud and crass disregard of the feelings and rights of others, lay a weakness which his manner was calculated to cover. Perhaps a fundamental lack of courage, a deep seated streak of saffron.

If so, it hadn't shown today. Jesse had taken unmerciful punishment and had handed out the same. And it seemed that he still had the will to try and get to his feet again, though lacking the physical ability to do so.

Then, as swiftly as it had come, that fleeting moment of respect left Larkin. For Jesse, his big shoulders still weaving and rolling, fixed his dazed glare on the empty holster at Larkin's side and understood the significance. He reached for his own gun.

It was a definite move, though made pawing and clumsy because of reactions clubbed far below normal speed. And Larkin, diving forward, got both hands on Jesse's wrist, driving it back and around. He got a knee between Jesse's shoulders for leverage and for a moment thought he'd dislocated Jesse's shoulder. The gun dropped from Jesse's fist, and with a cry that was hardly human, Jesse went face down in the dust of the trail. Larkin caught up the gun and staggered back.

Now it was done. Now the purpose and the need ran out of him, and he weaved about in front of his beaten enemy like a drunken man. He lurched up on his toes and teetered there, then dropped back on his heels and had to shuffle back a step or two to keep from toppling over.

His throat was raw, his lungs on fire, and it

seemed he just couldn't gulp in enough air to satisfy their craving. Sweat was a stinging salt slime across his face, and the raw taste of his own blood was on his tongue. Twice he scrubbed a forearm across his eyes, trying to clear them. Here was victory, but the price had been high.

Slowly balance and a measure of strength began to return. That terrible feeling of drained emptiness began to recede, and the labor of his lungs became less frantic. He grew conscious of the burn of the sun on his bared head and he began peering around for his hat. He saw it, off there to one side in the sage and when he moved to recover it, saw his lost gun lying beside it.

He still held the weapon he'd taken away from Jesse Schell, and now, with a sweep of his hand, threw it far out into the sage. He dropped his own gun in its holster and came back out into the trail. Jesse had rolled over, was up on one elbow. It took harsh effort on Larkin's part to get out his words.

"I showed you who owned the trail, Jesse. I showed you — !"

The words sounded stupid to Larkin, but at the moment he couldn't think of any better ones. The power of thinking, it seemed, had damned near been knocked out of him.

Down the trail a horse stamped, snorted restlessly. Larkin looked. It was his own horse, standing above dragging reins. He went for it, wondering why the trail was so uneven . . .

He gathered up the reins, then leaned against

the horse's shoulder for a moment before trying to get into the saddle. It took desperate, teeth gritting effort, but he made it. Off to one side, Jesse's horse stood in the sage.

Larkin rode back to the place of the fight. Jesse was on his knees now, pushing to get to his feet. He made it, and wobbled aside as Larkin rode past.

"That's right, Jesse," said Larkin thickly. "Get off the trail!"

Up ahead, Larkin saw Joyce Creager, half turned in her saddle, staring at him. He'd never seen her so white of face, so big of eye. He wondered why there should be moisture shining on her cheeks. He blinked. Couldn't be tears, could it? Why should there be tears, unless over Jesse? Wouldn't be on his account, that was for sure.

He pawed clumsily at his hat, and his words were blurting. "Don't cry over Jesse. He ain't worth it, Joyce. There's a streak in him. I always figured there was, and I brought it out. No, don't cry over Jesse. He'll still live to clutter up good range."

His words seemed to break some kind of a spell that had held Joyce all through the brutal, no quarter fight. She did not answer Larkin. She just whirled the fretting sorrel and let it run.

The Three Link headquarters stood in a spacious basin, cupped into the mighty flank of the Royales. Here Alec Creager had built a fine, staunch home for himself and his daughter. The ranchhouse was painted white and it held a cool sparkle against the background of several towering pine trees which formed a rough half circle about it.

Along one edge of the basin a creek ran, reaching for the valley, curving across the flats to the distant river beyond. And at one place the Three Link trail to town cut across this creek. By the time he reached this crossing, Britt Larkin was clear headed again, with much of his strength returned. But he was sore and beaten from head to foot and sight of the limpid creek waters decided him.

A little below the crossing and deep shrouded by willow growth was a sizeable pool. Larkin rode down to it, swung stiffly from the saddle, stripped and slid into the pool's depths. The water was cold and the first all-over touch of it made him catch his breath. After that, the caress of it was a healing balm.

He swam and drifted slowly back and forth and when, after a little while, he climbed out and dressed, the blood and dirt and sweat were washed away and vitality again coursed through him. Back again in the saddle, he headed on up the trail toward Three Link headquarters. And as he came up to the place he saw Alec Creager sitting in a cane bottomed chair on the wide veranda which ran all across the front of the ranchhouse. There was neither friendliness nor welcome in Creager's look and manner when Larkin stepped from his saddle and climbed the veranda steps. And Creager's first words were a crusty growl.

"What you trying to do, Larkin — set this whole damn range aflame?"

Larkin met the cattleman's stare. "Meaning what, Alec?"

"Proud of yourself, maybe, staging that kind of a dirty brawl in front of Joyce? She was all broken up when she got home."

Larkin kept silent while he twisted up a smoke. Then he said, "Sorry she had to see it, Alec. But there was Jesse, with the same old bully and brag. And I'd had all I could stomach of it."

"He marked you up some," said Creager, with something almost like satisfaction.

Larkin's jaw tightened. "Some," he admitted laconically. "But it was Jesse who had to get off the trail."

A glint of anger showed in Creager's frosty eyes. "You rode out here to brag about it, maybe? If so, I ain't got time to listen."

Larkin shook his head. "I came out to talk to you about squatters."

Creager banged both fists on the arms of his chair. "Damn the squatters! Be a great day for this valley when they're gone. Biggest mistake me and Jesse ever made was to let the first two or three families light at all down on the river flats. We might have known there'd be others to come in and join 'em. Now we got the chore of moving them all out."

"Wish you'd listen to me a little on that subject, Alec," said Larkin. "I'm hoping to get you to see those people in a little more generous light. I believe I can show you where they can do us both a lot of good."

Creager laughed harshly. "That's fool talk, Larkin. You'll never make me see them in any other light than as a damned blight on a good range." Creager got to his feet. "I got work to do."

"Then you won't even listen?"

"You heard me, didn't you? The only word I want on those squatters is that they've got the hell out of Reservation Valley. And that better be quick, or I'll make it my personal chore to see that they do. That answer enough for you?"

Larkin's face sharpened into hard lines. "It isn't the one I hoped to get. Just a little bit ago, Alec, you said something about setting this range aflame. Well, you can do that if you try and rough those people up. That applies to both you and Jesse Schell. Because it's my feeling those people won't stand to be pushed around any more. They're going to stick. And if you want a fight, you'll get one!"

"Think so?" jeered Creager.

"I know it!" said Larkin. "And I'll be in there, helping them. Now you have it, Alec. Cut and dried. Black and white."

Creager stiffened, reared up on his toes. For a moment Larkin thought the cattleman was going to swing a fist at him. Creager's eyes were blazing and his voice was a thick, erupting growl.

"A damned, lick-spittle coyote, Larkin, that's you! Taking sides against your own kind, over a flock of squatters. God damn it, ain't there any man in you at all?"

"There's too much man in me to allow a lock-brained fool like Jesse Schell do my thinking for me. Can you say the same, Alec?"

Larkin knew what he was saying, knew that this was waving the red flag in front of the bull. But he didn't care. Right at this moment he knew he was all through trying to appease Alec Creager, or to gain his support in any way. The thing that had risen in him when he forced Jesse Schell off the trail, now stood out in him again. He gave Alec Creager back stare for stare, yielding not an inch.

"That's it, Alec," he said. "If you want a fight, a fight you get. Think it over. You want dead men on the ground, that's where you'll find them."

He could see the blood throbbing in the veins of Creager's throat, at his temples.

"Get out!" Creager's voice was thick. "Get off this ranch. Don't ever come back. Get out!"

Larkin still held his ground, looking Creager up and down.

"I was wrong. Up until now, regardless of this and that, I held to the belief that you were a big man, a sound man. I was wrong, Alec. And I'm sorry. It's tough to have your respect for a man knocked to pieces."

Larkin turned away then, dropped down the

steps, went to his horse and headed off down the town trail again.

Alec Creager stood as he was, clenching and unclenching a pair of gnarled fists. His breathing was heavy and sharp, whistling a little through his nostrils. He was simmering with fury.

Steps sounded and Joyce came out of the ranchhouse door, crossed over and stood beside her father. Her face was pale and strained.

"I listened, Dad," she said simply. "I — I think I'm going to cry."

Creager whirled on her. "Cry! What for? Certainly not over that damned, traitorous whelp. He'd side with the squatters to fight me! Me, by God! Who's been his neighbor for years. I'll show him! Before I'm done with that fellow, he'll come crawling to me on his hands and knees. Fight me, will he!"

"But he won't, Dad. Britt will never crawl to you or anyone else. Can't you realize that?" Joyce's voice broke into a little wail and she caught at her father. "No, Britt will never crawl. He beat Jesse off the trail. I — I saw him do it, Dad. There was something about him at that moment, something dark and deadly. He'd have made Jesse get off the trail or — or he'd have killed him. I tell you I saw that in him. You — you must never fight Britt Larkin. I don't think I could bear having you and Britt fight. Oh, Dad — !"

She was crying, all right, her face buried against her father. Alec Creager, still taut and stiff with anger, hardly knew what to make of it.

"You cryin' over fear of my hide or of Larkin's?" he demanded heatedly. "Girl, just what are you drivin' at?"

She pulled away from him. "You — you just don't understand, Dad."

She turned and ran back into the ranchhouse.

Henry Castro had moved his bucket chair out on the porch of his store and was seated there in the shade of the overhang, looking out across the wide, sage matted miles of Reservation Valley. His hands were folded across his round little stomach. He turned his head and cocked an eye as Britt Larkin rode in, stepped from his saddle and came up on the porch with a hint of drag to his step.

"My God!" said Castro. "You change in looks every time I see you. What did you run into this time? Don't tell me you got worked over out at Three Link?"

Larkin shook his head. "Met Jesse on the trail. Jesse had his same old idea. The trail belonged to him. I couldn't see it that way. It was considerable argument, but Jesse got off."

Henry Castro whistled softly, studied Larkin more keenly. There was, he decided, something about the line of Larkin's jaw and something deep in his eyes that he'd never seen before. Something flinty and unyielding.

"So!" he murmured. "You put Jesse in his place, eh? Well, that's a blessing. Of course, you didn't get on out to see Alec Creager?"

"Yes," said Larkin. "I went on out to Three Link. I saw Creager."

"What luck did you have with him?"

"None at all." Larkin was silent while he built a smoke. "Afraid I've misjudged Creager all along, Henry. He's not as wide between the eyes as I thought."

"Oh, I wouldn't say that, Britt. It's just that Alec can be damned bull-headed when he wants to."

Larkin hunkered on his heels against the front of the store. His face was shadowed.

"I'm taking back that request for credit, Henry. I've no right to ask for it now, because there's a fight shaping up and I don't know how it will end."

"Hell, boy," said Castro quietly, "you didn't expect this big idea of yours to be just a waltz, did you? With a hair pin like Jesse Schell in the way, along with a pig headed old jackass like Alec Creager to clutter up the picture, too?"

Larkin's voice was tight. "Schell I can handle. I'd have no reservations with Jesse. I could and will throw a gun on Jesse if he gets too much in my way. I don't think I could do that with Alec Creager."

Henry Castro rummaged through his pockets, came up with a slightly tattered cigar. He broke off the worst end of this, lit the other end and puffed for a time in silence, his glance again running out across the heat clotted distances of the valley.

"Been thinkin'," he said finally. "More I think on it, the better I like your idea. For years I been runnin' this store, and while I've made a living and managed to lay a little money aside, you might say my business is in a groove and not a very deep one, either. The only thing that could make that groove deeper and broader is more people coming into Reservation Valley. When Alec Creager and Jesse Schell keep people out of this valley, they're hurtin' me."

Castro paused, took his cigar from his lips and waved it for emphasis. "I don't like that kind of a deal one damn little bit. Creager and Schell got no right to keep me a two-bit storekeeper, when I might become a dollar one. So, I've made up my mind to take the gamble. I'm gamblin' you're right when you say the squatters will stick, Britt. You still want that credit, you can have it. And to hell with Creager and Schell!"

Larkin came to his feet. "You really mean that Henry?"

"Damn right I mean it! Creager and Schell may think they're God and His helper. They ain't! I been checkin' things in my warehouse. I got some of the stuff you want, diggin' tools and some chain. You say so, I'll have it hauled out to the squatter camp today. And I'll order up the rest of the gear from Button Willow."

Larkin dropped a hand on Castro's shoulder, gripped it tightly. "Henry, I make you this promise. If we don't put this deal over, I'll still show you the best fight you ever saw."

"Boy," said Castro gently, "I don't stand too tall, and I'm kinda fat. But in my time I've licked a guy or two. Wait'll the next time I see Alec Creager. I'll blister his damned, cantankerous hide! Now, shall we round up a wagon and load what gear I got in stock?"

Larkin got the wagon and team at Bick Pennell's livery barn, and he and Henry Castro loaded it. As a final thought, Larkin turned to Castro soberly.

"You got four Winchesters on your rack, Henry. I'll take them, too, along with a case of fodder for them. Jesse Schell being Jesse Schell, we got to face realities. The squatters got some guns, but they could use more. We can't expect them to fight bullets with pick handles."

Castro reached for the rifles without argument. "I recollect an old saying, Britt. You can't make an omelette without breakin' eggs. If Jesse insists on it, he'll have to take the consequences."

Larkin drove the wagon out of town, his saddle mount at lead behind. From the wagon seat, Larkin could look far out across the miles of sage. Underneath that sage was earth, good, fat earth. Put water on it and all manner of useful things would grow. Earth, sun, water. Together they provided a magic alchemy out of which could lift a good and fruitful future.

In his mind's eye, Larkin saw that sage go, saw

the freshened, released earth turn green with ripe wealth; farms and fields, giving up long stored goodness.

He thought of Jesse Schell and Alec Creager, and grimness leaned his jaw. He thought of what Alec Creager had called him. A damned, lick-spittle coyote! He'd taken it from Creager, where he wouldn't have from any other living soul. But there were limits — !

He clucked to his team, hurrying it along.

The squatter camp was in something like a period of suspended animation; a little uncertain, yet anxious to get moving in some constructive direction. Cass Partee and Oake Calloway came hurrying up. At sight of the gear, Calloway's eyes gleamed.

"We can get to work!"

"If you've decided on the deal," nodded Larkin.

"We've decided! We called the whole camp together, Cass and I did. We laid your proposition in front of the folks. At first I thought it wasn't going to do any good. Then, as folks thought about it, the possibilities began to get hold of them. Some of us men took a walk up to the gorge and saw that it was possible to put up a dam and get water into that gulch. In the end, I reckon it were the women folks who put the clincher on. They said flat out they were plumb tired of the way things been goin' in the past. They yearned to stay put, have a decent, lastin' home for a change. So we put it to a vote — and we won! We're with you, Larkin!"

A smile softened the tension in Larkin's face. This was what he had hoped for, this was what he'd gambled on. Gambled everything. Now it didn't matter what Alec Creager had called him. Nor did the punishment he'd taken in the brawl with Jesse Schell.

"That's great, Mr. Calloway. Now what I got here are just the supplies Henry Castro happened to have on hand. He's ordering the rest of what we'll need from Button Willow. What we got here is enough to give you a start at clearing sage. That's the first requirement, anyway. Building the dam and running ditches can come later."

Looking over the load, Oake Calloway saw the four Winchesters and the case of ammunition. His expression sobered, and Larkin saw it.

"I never represented this thing to be easy, Mr. Calloway. It could come to a bullet throwing. If so, I don't want you people to be caught short of weapons. This you can count on. I'll be in any fight with you, all the way."

Oake Calloway's blunt jaw hardened. "A man can run away from his pride only so far, Larkin. After that he stands and fights. We're ready to."

The wagon unloaded, Larkin turned to Cass Partee. "Wonder could you get this rig back to Bick Pennell in town, Cass? Because I got a big chore coming up on my own range and I want to get right at it. I got a considerable herd of mixed, mongrel cattle to round up and drive out to

Button Willow. For I'm done with anything that isn't the best. I'm making a brand new start with Herefords, white faces, real beef stock."

"The rig will get back to town," Partee nodded. "This shapes up as a brand new start for everybody, doesn't it?"

"Something else," said Larkin. "Cass, you post guards at night. Don't take anything for granted. I'm hoping those guards will never see anything but the stars. Just the same, you post them!"

"They'll be posted," was the quiet promise.

Chapter V

GRIM FRUIT

BRITT LARKIN and the Dodd brothers, Chuck and Harley, rode the limits of Larkin's Tin Cup range. They rode the high parks, the timber gulches, the meadows and the aspen swamps which spread far up against the crest of the Royales. They bunched Tin Cup cattle and headed them down out of the mountains. Within a week, Len Revis joined them, a trifle more thin and gaunt than usual, but with most of the signs of the beating he had taken, faded out.

Hack Dinwiddie had come up to headquarters, his wagon loaded with his portable forge and kegs of horse shoes, and had shod the cavvy all around, and now these horses earned their new shoes as Larkin and his three riders virtually lived in their saddles.

It was dawn to dark toil. They slept where night caught up with them, ate frugal, hasty meals over small, guttering camp fires, stamped these out and hit saddle leather again. They cleaned Larkin's range from top to bottom.

Chuck and Harley Dodd were quiet-faced, reliable hands, men of early middle age, leathery and tough fibred, frugal of speech, expert with horses and cattle. Larkin had explained his future plans with them, before starting the roundup.

"It means we're going to be tied in tight with the squatters, boys. Their fight will be our fight. Which isn't going to make us a bit popular in some other cattle camps. You boys have a right to know that and to act on it according to your own ideas about such things."

The Dodd brothers had considered gravely, which was their usual way. Then Harley spoke for both. "It'll be an interestin' experiment. We'll dangle along, Chuck and me."

"Thought you weren't interested in too many profits," Len Revis had chided, when he got all the picture. "Now you're goin' all out and hell bent, aimin' to get rid of one herd and then bring in another."

To which Larkin had shrugged. "Maybe it's for the fun of trying out a new idea, Len. To sort of upset the accepted order of things."

"You always did talk about quality instead of quantity," agreed Len. "Hope we don't stub a toe. I try to be a fair minded man, but I ain't got the confidence in the squatters you have. My experience has turned them up as bein' sort of uncertain critters."

To which Larkin had drawn old Len over to an opening in the timber and pointed down toward the valley, where several pillars of smoke were lifting.

"Sage brush being grubbed out and burned, Len. Ground opened up. Those people aren't going to quit."

They bunched the herd and brought it down out of the timber and sent it in a long, dusty column across Reservation Valley. Here they saw small mountains of sage brush, piled and burning, the bright glow of flames beneath and climbing pillars of sooty smoke above. Len Revis twisted in his saddle and spat.

"Mebbe I been wrong about these folks. Got to admit they're showin' more git-up-and-git than any like 'em I ever saw before."

Leaving Len and the Dodd brothers to keep the herd moving, Larkin cut back along the river flats. He was startled at the size of the area already cleared. He saw men black with sweat and dirt and fire soot, digging and drubbing and chopping. He saw lengths of looped chain, with horses hitched at either end, drag out heavy yards of brush and haul it up to the fires.

Cass Partee came over, scrubbing sweat and dirt from his face. "How's it look?" he grinned.

"Great! Man, you people have been working."

Partee spat on his hands. "We've just started. Wait'll you see the finish."

They took the cattle down the long, slow, dusty miles from Reservation Valley to Button Willow. Larkin sent word ahead by stage and when the tired, bawling herd reached the loading pens at Button Willow, a line of slatted cattle cars were waiting.

Lean, sun blackened and weary, Larkin and his three riders began the loading job immediately, while a noisy, fussy little yard engine spotted empty cars and hauled loaded ones away.

Even darkness did not stop the job. Every moment of delay meant draining away a little more fat, and fat was money. So they worked with prod pole in one hand and a lantern in the other. All night long they kept at it, and saw the sun come up again through eyes sunken and red rimmed from fatigue. The air was thick with dust, with the smell of cattle and coal smoke and steam from the engine. But they had the last protesting steer into the last car before noon of that day, and less than an hour later an east bound freight picked up the cattle cars and took them, groaning and protesting, away into the hazy distance.

"Me," croaked Len Revis, "I want a drink, a meal, a bath and a bed. And if any hair pin wakes me up before I'm ready, then I haze that son-of-a-gun with a forty-five."

Len and the Dodd brothers went off together. Larkin spent half an hour in the station house, working out several messages concerning white faced cattle. And after he'd seen these messages go out over the telegraph wire, he went in search of the same things Len Revis had declared for.

They made much better time on their way

back to Reservation Valley, not being held down to the plodding pace of cattle. And on the day when, shortly after noon, they came through the low, southern pass of the valley, they saw over east, above Beaver Flats, the heavy smudge of smoke lying across a hot sky. Len Revis had his look and shook his head ruefully.

"Reckon I'll have to take back some of the talk I've made. For doggoned if they ain't still at it. Never did expect to see a flock of squatters put out that way. Give 'em a little more time and they'll have all the sage brush in the valley piled up and burned. Bet every time Jesse Schell gets a sniff of that smoke he likes to bust an artery."

Turning in to Fort Cord's single street, Larkin saw Alec Creager and Henry Castro standing on the store porch, looking toward the smoke and arguing. Len Revis and the Dodd brothers headed for the Guidon to wash the dust from their throats, but Larkin turned toward the store. He had no idea how Alec Creager would act when they met up again. He wanted no further words with Creager if he could help it, but neither could he dodge the man forever.

As Larkin came up on to the store porch, spur chains chuffing, Creager turned on him with a growled question.

"Just what the devil do your squatter friends think they're goin' to do, Larkin?"

Larkin shrugged. "Fairly obvious, isn't it? Clearing land of sage brush, so they can plant something worth while. And at my suggestion, just to keep the record straight."

"More and more I wonder just how crazy one man can get," said Creager. "I hear you've plumb cleaned out your herd. Sold it, hide, hoof and horn. You goin' out of the cattle business?"

Larkin smiled thinly. "Hardly. Something you and Jesse Schell can remember, just in case you get any ideas about my high park range."

Creager reddened angrily. "That's damn poor talk. I don't like it."

"Tough," shrugged Larkin. "You've never hesitated to throw poor talk my way. What leads you to think you're immune from the same?"

"Britt's got a point there, Alec," put in Henry Castro drily.

Larkin's smile became a mirthless grin. "Alec been telling you I'm a poor risk, Henry?"

"That's something I've already made my mind up on," Castro answered. "Alec knows just where I stand, there."

Alec Creager scuffed his boot heels restlessly. "I'm just tryin' to find out some straight answers. I don't want to see any real violence start. I don't want to see men cut down by gunfire, not even any of them damn squatters. For there's women and kids out there. But if the squatters are allowed to dig in and get set — ! Damn it, Larkin, just why are you so strong for them? If you'd stayed out of the argument, they'd be long gone, now. And I doubt I can keep Jesse Schell peaceful much longer."

"You better try," said Larkin, harshness

creeping into his tone. "The day Jesse jumps the traces and starts getting rough, that day he starts something he can't stop."

The old cattleman stared at Larkin, then glanced away. "You've cleaned out the herd you had. What do you aim to put in its place?"

"White faces," said Larkin. "There won't be many at first because that kind of high grade stuff costs money, big money. But they'll increase. I'm tired of working mixed, mongrel stuff. I'm tired of getting third grade prices for third grade beef. I'm tired of working all summer to put a little fat on even a third grade critter and then watching most of it drain off on the drive to Button Willow. I'm through sitting back and letting that sort of damn foolishness go on forever. So, I'm going at things different from now on."

"Me and others have done all right at it," snapped Creager.

"You mean you used to do all right at it," said Larkin. "Back in the days when your stuff was as good as anyone else's. Yeah, you made money then. But for the past half dozen years you've been grazing and handling three head of mongrel stuff to get the price one good white face would bring. So you haven't been making money during these years, you haven't been breaking even. I know it and you know it. All you've been doing is keeping up a front. That's all, while damning everything and everybody but your own pigheadedness. Because you can feel things slipping. Give you another ten years at the same sort of business and you'll end up a busted flush."

Larkin fully expected another outburst from Creager and was surprised when it did not show. Creager flushed, but his tone was reasonably even as he made retort.

"I know enough not to tie in with a bunch of squatters. They'll leave you high and dry and then laugh at you, Larkin. Then we'll see who's busted."

Creager stamped away, spare and angular, a chunk of granite steeped in old creeds and customs and lines of thinking; fighting change, unwilling to recognize or concede that change was bound to come, that it was inevitable.

"I'm amazed," murmured Henry Castro. "You really slapped the spurs to the old boy, Britt, and he more or less took it. Something's come over him. A month ago he'd have wanted your heart for that kind of talk."

"Kind of surprised me, too," admitted Larkin. "Last time I talked to him he was chock full of raw meat. You and he were having some kind of an argument when I came along, Henry. What about?"

Castro chuckled. "He was tryin' to find out if I knew what the squatters were really up to. I didn't show him any cards. Let the old maverick dangle a while. Do him good. How'd the drive come out?"

"Same old thing. Fat draining off the cattle all the way to Button Willow. That damn trail should be paved with silver dollars by this time. But we loaded every critter we started with. So I'll have some cash coming through pretty quick to slap against that account of mine."

"Huh!" grunted Castro, staring out at the drifting smoke haze again. "Did I say anything about wanting any cash? Save your money. You'll need it to buy that herd of white faces. I'll carry your credit as long as necessary. This is my fight as well as yours, now. I sent in the order for those Fresno scrapers and other stuff. It should be showing up in another week."

"Henry," said Larkin, "you revive my faith in mankind."

Larkin and his men stopped by at Beaver Flats on their way home. The air was thick with pungent smoke. In that smoke men toiled steadily with drag chains, axes and grubbing tools. Women and even some of the older children were busy, too, gathering up armfuls of brush missed by the big drags.

Cass Partee, black with soot and sweat, grinned up at Larkin. "Well?"

"You folks make me feel like a damned loafer," said Larkin. "The other tools and supplies will be along in another week. When they get here I'll be down here doing my share, Cass. We'll start on the dam and the ditches then. Any sign of trouble show up?"

Cass Partee hesitated. "Not exactly. But we're short of fresh meat and yesterday morning old

Jed Sharpe headed back up into the mountains to see if he couldn't pick up a couple of deer. He hasn't come back. We're getting a mite uneasy about him."

"This time of year the deer hang out pretty high up," said Larkin. "Sharpe probably got so far back he decided to lay out for the night. But the boys and I will keep our eyes open for him. And I'll see that you get some fresh meat. I left a few head of stock back on my range for just that reason."

Rose Calloway came by with an armload of brush. She gave Larkin that same direct, open smile. Larkin touched his hat.

"Makes me ashamed to see you women working like this."

She gave a quiet laugh. "Why not? Every woman craves a solid piece of earth where she can stay and build things about her. If she isn't willing to work for that, then she doesn't deserve it."

She went on with her chore, full of that strong, free grace.

The afternoon was running out when Larkin and his men jogged their weary broncs out of the timber and across the big park which held the Tin Cup headquarters.

"Seems pretty empty without a flock of critters grazin' around," said Len Revis. "But just give us time and there'll be little white faced bummers scamperin' all over this park, eh Britt?"

Before Larkin could answer, Harley Dodd

stiffened high in his saddle and his usual quiet drawl carried a bleak ring as he exclaimed, "Britt! You see what I see, hangin' from the ridge pole of the cabin?"

Larkin looked, swore softly and dug in the spurs. The rest raced after him. They pulled to a halt before the cabin and sat their saddles in a silent, grim faced half circle. The horses, jaded though they were, stamped and shifted nervously.

The ridge pole of the cabin projected a good four feet past the eaves. Over the pole a rope was slung, the free end carried down and lashed to a foundation log. On the other end of it hung a dead man, grizzled and gaunt and shrunken!

Save for the gusty breathing of the horses and the chittering bark of a squirrel cutting cones back in the timber, there was no sound. Then Len Revis let go in hard, unbelieving tones.

"Good God! Who — why — ?"

Britt Larkin spoke from the depths of a stunned bitterness. "It must be old Jed Sharpe, gone out to try for a couple of deer for the folks down on the flats. He was over-due back. This is why!"

They dismounted and cut the dead man down, laid him out there in front of the cabin. He was an old man with thin, gray hair. The front and back of his shirt was dark and stiff with dried blood. He'd been shot through. His ragged cotton pants were held up with make-shift leather galluses; his square toed, flat heeled, muchly worn boots were those of a man of the soil, not of the saddle.

"He was dead before they ever hung him up," said Harley Dodd. "The shot was what killed him." Harley straightened and turned away. "Chuck, you go east. I'll head west. Look for sign."

Harley and Chuck moved off, leading their horses, eyes searching the earth. Len Revis walked a savage circle.

"Only a damned human animal would do a thing like this. Killing the pore old feller was bad enough. But then to hang him up on a rope — !" Len smashed a clenched fist into the open palm of his other hand.

Larkin said nothing. He knew how Len felt, and his own anger became a couched and icy thing within him. For this was a grisly, macabre thing they had encountered. Here was the dark and shadowy start. Here in these deep hills was the beginning of a trail now certain to be wreathed in gun smoke. This was more than just a cruel and pointless killing. This was a grisly, flaunting challenge; ironic, cynical, savage.

Larkin finally spoke. "Catch up a fresh bronc, Len. Take the word down to the squatter camp. Tell Cass Partee and Oake Calloway. Have them bring a wagon up. I want them to see this just as we found it."

Len Revis led his tired mount over to the corrals. Soon he was spurring away on a fresh horse. Larkin went into the cabin, came out with a blanket and spread it carefully.

He looked around. The park lay empty and still, half gilded by the slanting rays of the sun, with blue shadows and mists hovering at the edge of the timber, ready to flow out and possess just as soon as the sun was fully gone. This was his home, and men had laid death at his door step.

The Dodd brothers had vanished into the timber, but presently it was Harley who came riding back. "Three horses went that way," he reported. "Looks like they cut for the summit after they got into the timber."

They put up their horses and while Harley was tending them, Larkin opened the cabin grub box and began putting some supper together. The sun went fully down and the shadows took over and a little twilight wind began to stir across the park. They got a light going and it was quite dark before Chuck Dodd reported. His words corroborated Harley's findings, but with added grimness.

"I found where they killed him. By the sign, there were three of them. The old feller had killed a deer and was packin' it out. Looked like he'd backed up to a down log to rest his load. That was when they shot him. Time musta been some time after noon yesterday. Because the coyotes had worked over the deer carcass considerable, last night. What did you find, Harley?"

Harley told him. "We'll pick up their trail in the morning."

It was a silent meal, each of them dropping back into the shadow of his own thoughts. The Dodd brothers were by nature quiet, taciturn men, who hid their feelings behind inscrutable faces. But Britt Larkin knew them thoroughly. They were hard working, sober, decent and reliable, and he knew that deep down inside they were as coldly angry and outraged as himself.

As they began cleaning up the dishes, Larkin said, "You know what this is the start of, boys."

Harley Dodd nodded. "We know. Mebbe we'll have considerable to say about the finish. When a man forfeits all rights, why then he's asked for what he gets. That goes for the three who did it."

It was a full two hours later before they heard the mutter of hoofs and the grind of wheels coming in across the park. Larkin lighted a lantern and went out. The wagon creaked to a stop before the cabin and Cass Partee, Oake Calloway and Sod Tremper climbed out. Sod Tremper had a rifle over his arm, one of the new Winchesters Britt Larkin had brought out to the squatters from Henry Castro's store.

Larkin pulled the blanket aside and held the lantern high. Sod Tremper cursed harshly. Oake Calloway spoke soberly, a little wearily.

"Jed Sharpe. Your man Revis told us some, Larkin. Mebbe you know more about it by this time?"

"There were three of them in on it," said

Larkin. "Sharpe was packing out a deer. He'd stopped to rest on a down log. That's when they shot him. After that they brought him here and hung him to the ridge pole of this cabin. We found him so when we rode in this afternoon. We've picked up their sign where they left. In the morning we follow it."

"I'd admire to go along," said Sod Tremper. "Jed was a lone man, like me."

"You had a claim, Sod," admitted Larkin. "But mine is a bigger one. They didn't kill Sharpe because they had anything against him personally. They did all this as a challenge to me. When they hung him to the ridge pole of my cabin it was as though they'd said, 'Well, here he is. What are you going to do about it?' That, they'll find out. They've been warned if they started anything rough, they'd get it rough. They will!"

The body was loaded into the back of the spring wagon. Larkin spoke a little awkwardly.

"I hope this won't turn you people against the big purpose. I don't need to tell you how bad I feel about it. In a way, I feel responsible, and —"

"How could you be, Britt?" cut in Cass Partee. "They found one of our people off alone and they killed him. You're no more responsible than I am, or Oake or Sod here. As for the big plan, don't worry. We gave our word and we stick by it."

"In the morning," promised Larkin, "there'll be a couple of pack horse loads of fresh beef brought down to your camp, to make up for the deer Jed Sharpe wasn't able to deliver."

They stopped over long enough for a cup of coffee and then the wagon rolled off. Larkin went immediately out to the corrals after a fresh horse.

"Where you headin'?" asked Len Revis. "Can't foller no sign in the dark, boy."

"I can find my way to Three Link," said Larkin. "Grab some supper and come along, if you want."

The way was due west, across some starlit park here, threading black aisles of timber there. When they crossed Wagon Creek they left Tin Cup range and moved on to Three Link ground. Half an hour later they cut around a timbered point and saw below them the lights of Three Link Headquarters. They slanted down into open meadows and presently pulled up by the shadowy line of corrals.

"I'll wait over at the bunkhouse," said Len Revis.

There was a hammock which hung at the end of the veranda of the ranchhouse. In the dark, Larkin was unaware that it held an occupant until he climbed the steps. Then came a stir and Joyce Creager's voice, asking, "Who is it?"

Larkin stopped, a little uncertain. He was recalling the last time he'd been face to face with this girl. There was, he thought, little chance of finding any friendliness here. He tried to keep his tone impersonal.

"Britt Larkin. I'd like to speak to your father. He around?"

She came out of the hammock and along the veranda. She had on some kind of light colored dress and she made a slim shadow against the dark.

"Dad's inside, with Tom Adin." Then she added, with a faint edge of hesitation, "I — I'm not sure you'll be — well —"

"Welcome," supplied Larkin. "Just the same, I've got to see him."

There was uncertainty here, decided Larkin, but no outright hostility, and he knew some satisfaction over that.

"Very well," said the girl quietly.

She led the way in, through a dimly lit hallway, then turned into a small corner room which Alec Creager used as an office. The cattleman, seated behind a paper littered table, came to his feet at sight of Larkin. Tom Adin, deep slouched in another chair, long legs stretched and crossed in front of him, noted the look on Larkin's face, stirred slightly and then went still again, though with a sharpening light in his eyes.

Alec Creager's opening remark was blunt. "Hardly expected this, Larkin, in light of what's passed between you and me the last couple of times we've met. What do you want?"

Larkin matched Creager's bluntness. "Wanted to tell you about a dead man. About a squatter, Jed Sharpe by name. When my men and I reached headquarters this afternoon we found Jed Sharpe hanging to the end of the ridge pole of my cabin. He'd been shot first."

Larkin heard Joyce Creager's smothered gasp, saw the start of surprise in Alec Creager. The cattleman stared at Larkin.

"Let me get this straight," he growled. "You mean to say this squatter had been shot, killed first, then hung up by the neck?"

"I mean just that."

"Surely you're not suggesting that I — that Three Link — ?" Alec Creager's words ran out on a rising note of truculence.

"Of course not," said Larkin. "I'm just telling you what I found."

Tom Adin spoke. "Any idea who, Britt?"

Larkin shrugged. "There were three mixed up in it. Chuck and Harley Dodd, after they'd done some prowling, agreed on that. And those two can read their sign. We're running the trail out in the morning."

"It won't lead to this ranch," said Creager, that harsh truculence still in his tone.

"I never at any time had the slightest thought that it would," said Larkin patiently. "You might kill a man, Alec. But you wouldn't shoot him in the back, and you wouldn't hang him by the neck afterwards. You're no ghoul. Neither are any of your men."

Somewhat mollified, Creager leaned forward. "Then why did you bring this word to me?"

"Just so you'd know that the lid is off and so you'll know who struck the first blow."

"You're pointin' the finger at somebody. If it ain't me, then it must be Jesse Schell. And Jesse wouldn't do a thing like that."

Larkin gave a small shrug. "I'm excepting only the Three Link."

"Until you know for sure, Larkin, I wouldn't name any man," warned Creager.

"I'll find the man, or rather, the men," Larkin said steadily. "And I'll name them. I'll find out if they acted under orders, and who gave the order. They're all equally guilty of a dirty, pointless murder. Then they threw that murder in my face. For that, we'll see."

Larkin made as if to leave and Tom Adin spoke up quickly.

"Just a minute, Britt. Yesterday, me and Cotton Barr were up near the summit, lookin' for strays. We were late gettin' out of there. We were giving our broncs a blow and having a smoke for ourselves before starting home. We saw, crossing a ridge below us, three riders. They were —"

"Hold it, Tom!" broke in Alec Creager. "This is no mix of ours. You don't know anything for sure. No, not our mix."

Tom Adin swung his head, fixed an intent glance on Creager. "You mean that, Alec?" he asked softly.

The tone was gentle, but there was something behind it and in Adin's eyes that made Creager squirm.

"Squatters never brought anything to a

country except trouble," growled Creager. He took a short turn up and down the room, with Tom Adin's questioning glance following him. Joyce was watching her father, too, her face strained and intent. Abruptly the crusty cattleman whirled.

"Hell, no!" he exploded. "Of course I didn't mean it, Tom. Murder is murder. Go ahead, have your say."

Tom Adin nodded, looked at Larkin. "The three Cotton Barr and I saw, were Obe Widdens, Duke Nulk and Clint Crowder. If that's worth anything to you, Britt, take it and welcome."

Larkin nodded. "Thanks, Tom. Seems there's been two or three things lately I've reason to thank you for."

Tom Adin stood up, reached for his hat. "A man calls things as he sees them," he said. "If he don't, he's a lost dog." He was leaving as he spoke, but paused for a moment beside a silent, pale Joyce Creager. He smiled down at her and his eyes were suddenly full of a warm affection. "Don't let this thing give you nightmares, young 'un." Then he was out a side door and gone, his spurs tinkling softly.

Larkin moved to leave, too. "Thanks for listening, Alec. I just wanted you to get the straight of this."

Creager nodded gruffly. "You're dead set on makin' this your fight?"

"That's right. Tom Adin just said everything. A man has got to call things as he sees them.

Good night!"

Joyce Creager wasn't satisfied with this. She followed Larkin outside, stopped him. "Did this Jed Sharpe have a wife, or children?"

"No, just friends. And the right to live."

She stiffened at Larkin's tone. "Of course. Did I suggest otherwise? I — I'm not callous."

"Sorry, Joyce," said Larkin, his tone gentling. "I know you're not. It's just that this affair has put a raw edge in me. You had to see it like I did to realize how it was. I didn't mean to be rough. I'd never want to be rough with you. Good night, Joyce."

For a long time after Britt Larkin and Len Revis had ridden away into the night, Joyce Creager stood there under the stars, knowing a chill that did not come from the breath of the night. There was a disturbing awareness that the secure and comfortable world she'd known for so long was somehow slipping away from her. With her own eyes, that day along the town trail when Britt Larkin and Jesse Schell had fought, she had seen raw violence explode in men, seen them meet in bloody, brutal conflict. Now more and worse of that same violence was leering past barriers beginning to crumble.

And things within herself were different. Emotions she had only vaguely considered, were loosening, to confuse and trouble her. The impact of events and the personalities of men were beginning to shake her. And beyond all, she had the uneasy feeling that her past sense of values hadn't been entirely sound. It was a sober, thoughtful girl who went back into the house.

Her father was still in his office, sunk in brooding thought. She put an arm about his shoulders and he reached up to take hold of her hand. There was a deep affection between father and daughter. When Joyce spoke, her words startled Alec Creager.

"There is no being neutral in this thing, is there, Dad?"

"Eh! Neutral? What are you driving at, child?"

"You just can't turn your back to a thing and make it cease to exist," was Joyce's sober statement. "You just can't tell yourself that something didn't happen, and know that it didn't. Britt said his men found sign to show there were three who did that — that awful thing. And Tom Adin said that he and Cotton Barr saw —"

Alec Creager pulled her down on his knee. "You just forget the whole thing. This is the business of men. Leave it up to them. I don't want you gettin' yourself all upset over something that doesn't concern you, lass."

Joyce shook her head slowly. "It isn't as easy as all that, Dad. There's been too much of that in my life, not concerning myself about others, I mean. Oh, I know you've meant it well, and I'm not blaming you in any way. But for too long I've lived in a world all padded with lovely, soft pink cotton. I'm not that fragile. I think it's high time I slept on some bare boards for a change."

Creager was startled, bewildered. "What in

blue blazes is that kind of talk? Time you slept on bare boards! Good Lord, girl, are you well?"

"Perfectly. I guess I make things sound kind of mixed up. Well, I am mixed up, and I've got to think about it. Good night!"

She leaned over, brushed a kiss against his cheek and left him.

Alec Creager stared at the door which closed behind her. His frosty brows were pulled into a troubled scowl.

"Pink cotton — bare boards!" he mumbled. "What's got into the girl?"

Chapter VI

TANGLED TRAILS

THEY LOST the sign far up along the summit of the Royales, where the cap rock broke through, gray and flinty and barren except for an occasional pocket where ragged snow brush and a few stunted, storm-beaten aspens clung.

This was well west of the Three Link range, was in fact due north of the eastern portion of the Running S range, where the last of the bigger high parks lay. Further along the Royales the timber took over more thickly and in that country were only a few scattered, isolated layouts, one man outfits for the most part, like those of Bob Watrous, Abe Dickshot and Pete Skene.

These men seldom left the deep hills. Only when they brought out their small scrubby shipping herds on the way to Button Willow, or when they drifted into Fort Cord with a pack horse or two after supplies from Henry Castro's store, were they seen in Reservation Valley.

In the lee of a ragged outcrop of cap rock, Britt

Larkin reined in his horse, pulled his neck deeper into the collar of his old, use-scuffed leather jacket. At this altitude there was a frigid bite to the drift of the high mountain wind, even though the sun was clear and well lofted.

"No use," he said. "We could run around up here for a week and still be no wiser than we are now."

Harley Dodd nodded agreement. There was just the two of them. Len Revis and Chuck Dodd were back on the home range, at the work of slaughtering a beef and taking the meat down to the squatter camp. Harley squinted into the far distance.

"We could drop in on the Running S, ask some damned pointed questions and maybe trip one of those jingos into an admission of some sort. So far we just know something we can't prove."

Larkin nodded. "We'll try it."

They went down from the cap rock to the timber benches below. In the far depths of the valley, smoke laid long drifting banners of smudge. The squatters had their brush fires going. This Jed Sharpe affair hadn't stopped them. Larkin spoke a little tightly.

"We got to go all the way through with this, Harley. Those folks down in the flats believe in us."

They threaded the timber benches, dropping in long slants across the curving flank of the mountains. They hit open park country and lifted their mounts to a swinging jog. And from the point of an angling ridge they finally looked down on a timber rimmed flat where buildings and lines of corral fences marked Jesse Schell's Running S headquarters.

They came in on the Running S past a corner of the corral area and saw Jesse Schell. He was leaning against the saddle pole by the cavvy corral gate, talking with two riders whose horses stood hip-shot and relaxed. These two were Alec and Joyce Creager.

Harley Dodd exclaimed softly. Larkin said nothing, but his shoulders stiffened.

Jesse Schell pushed away from the saddle pole, spread his feet and swung his heavy shoulders belligerently as he squared around to face Larkin and Harley. The passing days had erased most of the signs of Larkin's fists, except for the cut on his cheekbone. There was still a patch of bandage over this. In his eyes was a settled glare of open hatred.

Larkin's first attention was on Alec Creager, and the question in his glance brought a faint flush to the cattleman's leathery face. That same question was there when Larkin moved his glance on to Joyce. She met it with a quiet steadiness and Larkin touched his hat. Then he looked at Jesse Schell, and his question was blunt.

"Widdens around, or Clint Crowder, or Duke Nulk?"

"Maybe, maybe not," growled Jesse. "What's it to you?"

"Got a few questions to ask them."

"What about?"

Larkin's eyes held a boring chill. "You know. About a dead man, hung on the end of a rope to the ridge pole of my cabin."

"Maybe they're not interested."

"They better be. Harley, take a look in the bunkhouse. If they're in there, rout 'em out!"

Harley stepped from his saddle. Jesse Schell pushed further away from the saddle pole, barring his way.

"Take it slow, Dodd! You and Larkin seem to be forgetting whose land you stand on. Mine! Nobody prowls these premises without my permission. And you ain't got it!"

Alec Creager made an impatient, cutting motion with his hand. "Unbow your neck, Jesse. You've been telling Joyce and me you didn't know anything about this killing. When you act this way it makes me wonder. I think Larkin's suggestion is a good one. I'd like to hear what Nulk and Crowder and Widdens have to say for themselves."

Jesse Schell still held his ground. The man would always be like that, thought Larkin. Right or wrong, once he'd taken stand, Jesse would try and make it stick. Like an obstinate bull. Bound to stay put, pawing and bellowing, without rhyme or reason.

Alec Creager leaned forward in his saddle, putting the full weight of a deepening anger on this big, blonde, sullen faced man.

"Jesse, do you always have to play the part of a damned thick-headed fool? If those men are in the bunkhouse, get them out here. Else I'll go after them myself!"

Jesse tried to meet and hold Creager's anger, failed, so swung around and yelled.

"Obe, Clint, Duke! Come out here!"

More than a trifle startled at Alec Creager's flat stand, Larkin glanced at him. Meeting the look, Creager said, "You were ready to jump at conclusions when you rode in, Larkin. Not a safe habit, you see. For you could be wrong."

Widdens was the first to show. He came out of the bunk house slouchy and lank, a glinting wariness in his eyes. Duke Nulk was next, thick, burly, frowsy. Then came Clint Crowder, small, neat and cat-like. All had guns strapped on. Particularly did Widdens and Nulk put their open hostility on Britt Larkin.

They would always remember that night in town, when the hammering fists of this lean, brown faced man had battered them down. For him their hate was a deadly thing that nothing short of his death would appease. But because that same night had taught them something of Larkin's capabilities, they did not now let their hate override their caution.

Not so with Clint Crowder. His voice was as small and neat and purring as its owner and there was defiance in his every move and look.

"What's pushin' up the leaves, Jesse?"

"Come over here!" ordered Jesse Schell. Then his tone ran heavily sarcastic. "Mister Larkin here says he wants to ask you some questions.

We mustn't disappoint him."

"Questions about what?" purred Crowder.

Larkin shot it right at him. "About where you were day before yesterday. What were you and Nulk and Widdens doing over around my headquarters?"

"We weren't," mocked Crowder. "We don't crave the company of any squatter lover, so why should we go anywhere near his layout?"

Duke Nulk laughed coarsely. "Now ain't that pure gospel!"

Obe Widdens said nothing, but there was mockery in the hard shine of his eyes.

"Satisfied, Larkin?" jeered Jesse Schell.

Larkin did not answer him, did not look at him, but kept his attention strictly on the three Running S riders.

"His name," said Larkin with cold distinctness, "was Jed Sharpe. He came up into the hills from the squatter camp, looking for a deer. He killed one and was packing it out on his back. He stopped to rest on a down log. Some kind of sneaking human vermin shot him from behind. Then they carried him to my headquarters and hung him to the ridge pole of my cabin. Anything about that sound familiar to you three?"

"Why should it?" sneered Clint Crowder. "We weren't there."

Duke Nulk let go with his coarse laugh again. "Who'd go to all that fuss with a damned squatter?"

Again Jesse Schell jeered. "Satisfied, Larkin?"

"No! Not satisfied at all. But I can see how it is. You'd all swear to a common lie. I figured you would."

Clint Crowder shifted swiftly. "Lie, is it? Now there's a word I don't like, don't like at all. I never let any man throw it at me and I never will. It's a word you can take back, Larkin. Or eat. Right now!"

Crowder was moving in as he spoke, to stop only a short stride from Britt Larkin's horse.

Obe Widdens said, "Hah!" in a droning way and shifted a little further to one side.

Harley Dodd, when Jesse Schell called the three men from the bunkhouse, had swung into his saddle again. Now his words hit out sharply.

"Stay right there, Widdens! You too, Nulk!"

Harley had a gun in his hand and nobody had seen him draw it. There was more to taciturn, still-faced Harley than first met the eye.

At Harley's ringing order to Widdens and Nulk, Clint Crowder's glance flicked and shifted slightly, which was a mistake he had no chance to rectify. Crowder was wearing a beaded buckskin vest. Larkin grabbed, got a handful of the back of the vest, jerked it up, hauling Crowder completely off his feet, where he hung, spitting curses and unable to get at his gun because the lifting twist of that fancy vest had his arms pulled up and trapped.

Larkin gave the little rider no time or chance to pull free. He locked his free hand in

Crowder's hair, gave an upward, two-handed heave and hauled Crowder across the saddle in front of him, where he held him with one hand, while with the other he lifted Crowder's gun and threw it aside. Then he gave the raging little rider another lift and shove and sent him on over, where he hit the ground heavily on his face and chest.

It hadn't taken long, just a few seconds of swift action, with Larkin's horse whirling and half rearing. It was over and done with before anyone could interfere. Larkin quieted his horse and his words ran brittle.

"My patience is getting awful thin, Jesse. This thing I came about, I'll get at the bottom of before I'm done. When I do I'll write an answer. In the meantime, I'm laying out a dead line. It runs from Three Link headquarters due south across the valley through town. Running S stays west of that line. That means you and every man you got working for you. That's the line, from Three Link south through town. Don't forget it!"

Clint Crowder had pulled himself to a sitting position. He had met up with the ground, hard. His mouth was bleeding, his eyes dull and stupid from the shock. Larkin gave him a glance, then looked at Alec Creager.

"I made a wrong guess about you just now, Alec. Sorry. It's a habit I got to get rid of. All right, Harley!"

They swung their horses away, half circling, so

that at no time were their backs fully to Jesse Schell or his men. Schell stared after them and the inner workings of the man's mind and character lay fully exposed in his congested face in this unguarded moment. He turned, half lifted a hand as though to order Obe Widdens and Duke Nulk into some hostile move, but stopped this as Alec Creager's voice hit out.

"Let be, Jesse! They rode in, they looked you in the eye, they told you off. That was the time to do something, while they were looking at you. Larkin was right. There's a lot of lies around here. I think I'm fully convinced. Come on, Joyce!"

They turned their horses and rode away. Soon like Britt Larkin and Harley Dodd, they were out of the flat and into the timber.

Jesse Schell began to curse, low at first, then with a rising fury. Obe Widdens came over to him.

"Duke and me can make a fast ride around, Jesse. We can come in on the trail ahead of Larkin and Dodd. We can lay out and wait for them and —"

Jesse Schell swung a powerful arm, knocking Widdens to one side. "Shut up!" he snarled thickly. "You'll do nothin' until I tell you to. Get out of my way!"

He headed for the ranchhouse, almost staggering with rage. Obe Widdens stared after him, strange lights in his eyes. Then he shrugged and went back to the bunkhouse, with Duke Nulk rolling his thick, heavy legged way after him. None of them paid any attention to Clint Crowder, who got shakily to his feet, scrubbing a shirt sleeve across his bleeding mouth.

Crowder looked long in the direction Britt Larkin and Harley Dodd had gone. Then he looked at the ranchhouse, where Jesse Schell had disappeared. Finally he looked at the bunkhouse.

"I step out, ready for a play," he mumbled. "And they let me dangle. Schell, Widdens, Nulk — they dogged it, they wouldn't back my hand. I'll never go out on a limb for this damned outfit again. But Larkin, I'll take care of that bucko in my own way!"

He searched around for his gun, found it where Larkin had tossed it, picked it up and began wiping it off. Then he headed for the bunkhouse, a small man. Pale-eyed. Deadly.

The smoke of burning sage brush was a constant acrid fog against the sky. Over the miles from Button Willow to Fort Cord a big double hitch freight outfit came ponderously rolling, the twelve mule team plodding stoically, hame bells of the leaders chiming a thin, cheerful note across the sage. The sound of these brought Henry Castro to the porch of his store and he was there when the outfit rolled into town and came to a halt. The skinner climbed down from the high box.

"Lot of gear for you," he told Castro briefly.

"Where you want it?"

"Out in the valley," Castro said. "I'll show you."

Castro locked up his store, got a buckboard and team at Bick Pennell's livery barn, then drove out across the valley ahead of the freighter. When they pulled in at the river flats the squatters gathered around. Henry Castro, who had marked the extensive area already cleared, looked at these grimy, sweat stained men with a new respect in his eyes.

"I'm Castro," he said. "I run the store in town. Here's the gear Britt Larkin promised you."

He marked the quiet enthusiasm with which they helped the skinner unload, the shine in their eyes as they inspected the pair of Fresno scrapers and other tools. He watched women and children carrying armfuls of brush to the fires. After the unloading was done and the freighter headed back to town, Castro still lingered. Oake Calloway came over to the buckboard.

"You're helping Britt Larkin get this gear for us," said Calloway shrewdly. "It's business for you, I know. But I think there's another reason. Am I right?"

Castro nodded. "This valley's been empty long enough. Time it grew something else besides sage brush. You people have already done quite a chore."

"Just the start," said Calloway with satisfaction. "You'll see the day, Mr. Castro, when there'll be green fields."

"I doubted you folks at first," admitted Castro. "I didn't think you'd stick. Now I know you will. You'll be needing flour and other supplies. You run short of money, I'll carry your credit. I see you now as a sound risk."

When Castro got back to town he found Jesse Schell stamping up and down the porch of the store.

"Where the hell you been?" demanded Schell impatiently. "A man runs a store, he ought to keep it open."

Castro, about to slide a key into the lock, paused and looked Schell in the eye. "Don't use that tone on me," he said curtly. "Hell with you! You don't like the way I run my store, go some place else. As for where I've been, I just returned from delivering a lot of gear to those people out along the river flats. I don't suppose you like that, either?"

Jesse Schell flushed. "Long as you ask, no, I don't."

"Then," Castro told him bluntly, "you'll just have to lump it!"

He unlocked the door and went in. Schell, after glaring at the empty doorway for a moment, tramped heavily in behind him. In what was meant as a placating tone, Schell grumbled, "Ain't like you, Henry, to be on the peck this way. You act like you had a burr under your saddle blanket."

"Maybe I have," retorted Castro. "And maybe I'm galled raw. Because for too long this valley has been like a desert, just to suit the convenience of you and Alec Creager. You haven't given a damn for anybody but yourselves. Fellows like me and Hack Dinwiddie and Rick Pennell, we could just scratch along, barely making half a living instead of the full one which more people in the valley and town would mean. Just so nothing disturbed the setup you and Creager wanted to keep. Well, other folks beside you two have rights in this world. That's a fact you better wake up to."

The old, cornered bull look came over Jesse Schell. "Squatters don't rate," he growled. "Never did and never will. That's my final word."

"Then," said Castro acidly, "you better get along. Because you're talkin' to the wrong man." He turned toward the little corner cubby which served as his office.

"Wait a minute," blurted Schell. "I came in here to buy something. I want some Winchesters. And some ammunition."

"Right now I'm out of both," said Castro. "You take a look at the rack you'll see it's empty."

Jesse Schell looked. "What happened to those rifles? Last time I was in here there were four of them."

"That was then," shot back Castro. "Now is now." He went on in to his office.

Jesse Schell's eyes congested, his bull neck swelled. His voice lifted to something just short of an infuriated yell. "Maybe you sold them to the squatters? Well, they won't do that damned outfit any good. I'll — !"

Henry Castro slammed the door of his office, sat up to the desk. Jesse Schell stood for a moment, his head swinging back and forth. Then he cursed hoarsely, turned away and lunged out into the street, heading for the Guidon. There he ordered up a bottle of whiskey and a glass and retired with these to a corner poker table. He had a vast capacity for liquor and he lowered the level of the bottle swiftly.

For a full hour he sat there, wrapped in black thought, thought which carried him back over the past several weeks. He saw the picture as it had been then, and as it was now. And the grinding realization came to him that over those weeks, despite all he could do, things had moved steadily against him.

The sentiment he had relied on wasn't turning out right at all. Not even with Alec Creager. Yeah, even Creager was backing away, going soft toward those damned squatters. And he, Jesse Schell, was being left to play a lone hand.

The more he drank and thought, the blacker Jesse's thoughts became. This thing was no longer just a matter of rooting up a flock of squatters and running them out of the valley. The big issue in front of him now was Britt Larkin. Larkin! God, how he hated that man!

Jesse's big hands, spread flat on the poker table, clenched and unclenched, then clenched again. It was as though he were crushing something, squeezing the life out of it. Larkin! Jesse gulped another stiff drink.

But Britt Larkin wasn't a lone figure, now. In a showdown the squatters would back Larkin's hand. And, in all probability, Alec Creager might step in. And all that was too much to take on by himself. It all added up to the fact that he, Jesse Schell, had to have help in this thing. Help, from where?

It came to him out of nowhere, the idea. It brought him up straight in his chair, put a certain animal eagerness, a ruthlessness in his heavy face. Why not? If Alec Creager was no longer for him, then he was against him. And if he had to tear Creager down, so that he could get at Larkin — why not?

Jesse slammed a heavy fist on the table top, took a final drink, got up and left the Guidon. His heavy, thrusting stride was perfectly steady. Only the hectic flush in his face and a certain reddish tinge in his eyes showed the amount of whiskey he'd taken on.

He headed for home, pushing his horse to a foaming, trembling exhaustion. At headquarters he did not even bother to unsaddle the beaten animal, just swung down, lifted a heavy yell for Obe Widdens, then tramped on into the ranchhouse.

Widdens came slouching in. Schell met him with a question.

"Remember Dutch Klymer?"

Widdens relaxed a little, nodding. "Yeah, what about him?"

"Think you can locate him?"

Widdens got out tobacco and papers, twisted up a cigarette. "Maybe. Last I heard of Dutch, he was hanging out around Indio, across the mountains. If he's still in that region, reckon he could be found."

"Good! Roll yourself a pack and head for Indio," ordered Schell. "Find Klymer and tell him now's the time to make good on that threat of his. Tell him that Alec Creager is ripe for the picking!"

Obe Widdens went very still, blowing a thin blue line of smoke from pursed lips. "I don't get it, Jesse. I thought us and Creager —"

"Then you thought wrong," broke in Schell harshly. "So did I, for a while. I thought Creager would be with me, all the way. But he ain't. He turned soft about those damned squatters. He's turned soft towards Larkin. So, he's no good to me at all, now."

"I still don't get the angle of Klymer," said Widdens. "What good will it do us to turn him loose on Creager?"

"Start thinking," growled Schell. "Larkin will stick by the squatters and they'll stick by him. Running S ain't strong enough to handle that combination alone. With Creager siding us, yes. But Creager won't side us, now. In a showdown, I wouldn't put it past him to side Larkin and the squatters against us. I tell you, Creager has changed. So, we need help. We need Dutch Klymer."

Widdens considered this. "You're not goin' to get Dutch across the mountains without makin' it worth his while."

"Don't expect to," said Schell. "Who was it that originally run Klymer off this side of the Royales? Alec Creager. Klymer made the vow that some day he'd come back. Maybe that vow don't mean as much now as it did then. But I'm gambling that I can stir Klymer up again. He's bound to still hate Creager. So, I make him a proposition. He helps me handle the squatters and Mister Britt Larkin, then I help him put the squeeze on Alec Creager."

Obe Widdens dragged in another deep inhale, took the cigarette in his fingers and stared at the tip of it. "I thought Creager was your good friend, Jesse. You don't care how rough you get, do you?"

Schell swung a clenched fist in a violent gesture. "Just one thing I know for sure. If a man's a friend of mine, he's for me. The day he ain't for me, then he's no longer my friend."

Widdens argued cautiously. "Alec Creager may not be for you, but you ain't certain he's against you. But you sure will put him against you, for good and for ever, if you bring Dutch Klymer back on this range."

"Let him be as he damned pleases," said Schell. "It won't do him any good. He can't buck me and Klymer together. We'll take all the snort and smoke out of him."

"There's another angle," persisted Widdens. "How do you know we can't handle the squatters and Larkin, too, just by ourselves? We haven't really put much pressure on either of them, yet."

Schell scoffed profanely. "What the hell good did it do to kill that guy Sharpe and hang him up in front of Larkin's cabin? That was your idea, remember? A little of that treatment and the squatters would clear out in a hurry. That's what you said. Well, who's causin' all that smoke across the valley? I don't see any squatters runnin'. They're diggin' in, deeper all the time. And they got guns. Henry Castro, damn him, sold them every Winchester he had in his place. So it'll take man power to root out the squatters this time, and right now we ain't got it. As for Larkin, you and Nulk didn't do too well with him, as I remember."

A dull flush touched Obe Widdens' cheeks. "How well did you do with him, Jesse?"

Widdens braced himself for an explosion of rage on Schell's part. It didn't come. Jesse Schell just stared off into space, while he opened and closed one fist slowly and meaningfully. And, ruthless as Obe Widdens was himself, the look that settled and grew in Jesse Schell's eyes sent a chill through him.

"Go roll that pack, Obe," said Schell. "Find Dutch Klymer. Tell him it will be a wide open game, no limit!"

Chapter VII

THE WORKS OF MAN

THE JOB of clearing and burning sage went on. But men were busy at other tasks also, now that they had been supplied with tools and material. Up in the Saber River gorge above the falls, Britt Larkin and Oake Calloway and Cass Partee worked out levels and ran lines. And when they were satisfied with these there began the hard, grinding toil of battling solid, gray rock.

All day long the clank of sledge hammer on steel rock drills beat out a metallic cadence. From time to time the roll of exploding blasting powder drifted down Reservation Valley. Oake Calloway made up the powder charges, loaded the drilled holes, set off the blasts. And after each of these there were heavy rock fragments to be pried and lifted and cleared away. Then it was sledge and drill again, before could come another shattering blast. Stubborn men against stubborn rock and the men and powder slowly winning.

Up in the first edge of the timber on the

Royales, Len Revis and Chuck and Harley Dodd swung axes and pushed and pulled on a cross cut saw. They stacked logs of various lengths and thickness and they helped a squatter load these on a heavy work wagon to be hauled over to the gorge.

Along the slope of the valley, men and horses and a pair of Fresno scrapers furrowed the earth into an irrigation ditch which curved gradually down to the flats. On these flats women cooked food, carried it to the men. They washed clothes and they helped with the clearing and burning of sage brush. Everybody worked.

All his life Britt Larkin had been a saddle man, but he found a fierce, satisfying pleasure in toiling alongside of these people at a type of physical labor he'd never tackled before. Because all this was the building of the thing he'd so long had in mind and had planned. It was a big thing to see the plan taking shape. He sweated down to tempered rawhide and his hands grew callused and rough.

He found that a man could lose himself completely in a job like this. Days could slide by almost unnoticed and time was measured only in land cleared and rock moved and foot by foot progress made. Jed Sharpe's death had not been forgotten. Atonement for that would come in the future. Just now there was work to be done while the season was right.

So the hot summer days slid by and became weeks, with no let up in the driving work. From time to time Henry Castro drove out from town in his buckboard. The stout little storekeeper became a familiar figure and the squatters liked to see him. It was understood now by everyone how Castro had supplied his backing to the job.

He was continually marveling at the driving purpose and enthusiasm the squatters showed, and one day, up in the gorge, he told Britt Larkin so.

"Just goes to show how a man can be mistaken, if he gets in the habit of making snap judgement. Damned if these people ain't tremendous, Britt."

Larkin, putting aside a sledge hammer and scrubbing the sweat from his face, nodded.

"All of that, Henry. It boils down simply to the promise of a decent future. Consider the average squatter as we've known him in the past. He didn't have the heart to put too much effort into a piece of land, because he never knew when somebody like Jesse Schell would show up and force him to move on. He didn't dare set his roots too deep, because of the misery that would come with tearing them up. But these people can see permanence here, and they're willing to work until they drop to gain it. Things are really moving, Henry. By fall there'll be water on that land down yonder. A year from now — !" Larkin waved a hand. "Getting a run for your money?"

"Plenty!" asserted Castro. "Kind of feel I'm a part of all this, and it gives me more satisfaction than anything I ever did before. Any outside trouble lately?"

Larkin shook his head. "I laid out a dead line, and so far Jesse Schell has observed it. But I'm not deluding myself there. One of these days Jesse will come busting across it, full of trouble. He's too bull headed to learn anything other than the hard way. But we won't be caught unawares. I got old Sod Tremper on the prowl all the time, watching the trails, checking the signs. In the meantime, we're getting all the work done we can."

"Jesse Schell!" said Castro. "There's a man I've become sick and tired of."

Larkin grinned wryly. "Jesse just can't quit pushing and shoving. Given time, everybody gets tired of that sort of thing."

Not only had Larkin seen nothing of the Running S since he'd laid down the deadline, but he'd seen nothing of Three Link, either. And that bothered him some. From the very first it had been his hope to swing Alec Creager over to his idea, but so far he'd been unable to make any progress in that direction.

He did know, however, that the killing of Jed Sharpe had jarred Creager, plenty! And he knew that fundamentally, Alec Creager was a thoroughly decent man. But he was opinionated, set in his ways. A man like that was hard to move, for he hated to admit he'd been wrong in his estimate of other men and in his judgement of their motives.

It was noon of another day. Work had paused while men fortified themselves with food against the long, driving afternoon hours ahead. The food had been brought up by Rose Calloway. Now she was sitting cross-legged beside Larkin and Cass Partee while they ate.

Larkin had seen considerable of Rose since going actively to work with the squatters, and his respect and admiration of her had grown each day. She was always the same, this sturdy, wholesome girl of the earth. Her ready smile was open and sincere, with never a sign of coquetry.

The clothes she wore were old and simple, but habiliments of sack cloth could not hide her natural grace and beauty. She brought quiet satisfaction to a man, just by being near him. She laughed readily and the companionship she offered was free and natural.

But there was one thing which Larkin couldn't help noticing. That ready smile which she gave to everyone, held something special when she showed it to Cass Partee; a certain warmth which added a shine to her eyes.

Sober thought brought Larkin to the realization that this was as it should be. They were of a type, these two, made for the earth, rather than for saddle leather. These people might stand with their faces upturned to the sweetness of fresh falling rain, but they would seek the shelter of stout walls when the real storm winds blew and be content to cling to a fireside until the sun shone warm again.

They would never understand the lure of the action and freedom which a seat in a speeding saddle could give; they would not understand the basic spirit of adventure this seat held. The earth was their destiny, and they would only be happy when close to it. But they were clean strain, these two, and would do to tie to.

Oake Calloway, eager to be back at the job again, called Cass Partee over to help decide on the placement of another blast hole. Larkin, watching Rose Calloway's glance follow the wide shouldered young squatter, murmured softly.

"Just about the luckiest scoundrel I know, Cass is."

He saw the ripe color whip through her cheeks, but her eyes were quite steady as she looked at him. "I wouldn't know about that lucky part, Britt. But Cass is my kind and we understand each other."

Larkin grinned, teasing her. "Girl, as the old saying goes, your wisdom is only exceeded by your good looks. Now if you'd selected a shiftless hombre like me —"

She met his mood in like fashion, laughing softly. "I wouldn't have had a chance. I know my limits."

There was the click of a hoof on rock behind them. Rose turned her head, got quickly to her feet. "You've got a visitor, Britt."

Larkin came around and saw Joyce Creager sitting her saddle quietly a few yards away. He went over to her swiftly.

"Joyce! Say, this is fine! Get down and rest your saddle." Then, as another thought struck him, he asked, "Nothing wrong, is there? Everything all right over at Three Link?"

She did not answer as she dismounted slowly, looking sober and a little tired. Change had come over this girl. There was still that pride in her but there was a hint of shadow behind her eyes. She was watching Rose Calloway gather up the food containers and trudge away. Then she spoke quietly.

"She's lovely, isn't she?"

"Eh!" said Larkin. "Oh, you mean Rose Calloway? Yeah, she's great, Joyce. There are a lot of values in all these people. Workingest folks you ever saw. All of them."

She looked at him, sweated down to brown rawhide. "You've hardly been idle yourself, have you? What is this thing you're all slaving over? "What's the big purpose?"

Larkin told her. He explained the plan of the dam, of the channel being blasted through solid rock, and how the water would flow down across the valley slope to the thirsty land below. He told of feed crops that would be planted and harvested and of the feed pens for cattle that would be built, all along the drive trail to Button Willow and the railroad.

"No more trail worn, scrubby cattle for me," he ended. "The next cattle I put in at Button Willow are going to be white faces, and they'll be fat cattle, good enough to bring top market prices."

"And that is why you've sided with the squatters, Britt?"

"Partly. I admit to a certain selfish interest. I couldn't put the plan into effect by myself. I had to have the help of folks like these. They'll profit and so will I. So will your father if he'll join up with us." Then he added gravely, "But I always have recognized the fact that people like these squatters have rights, too. They're entitled to their share of the earth."

Joyce was silent for a little time, staring off into the day's heat haze. "I can see it," she admitted. "Green fields instead of sage brush. And though I've never been down the drive trail to Button Willow, I can see that, too. What it is like now and what it will be like when your plan is all done and working."

Larkin showed a wry grin. "Things are getting better. I got Henry Castro sold on the idea. Now I have you seeing it. If I could only get your father to open his eyes —"

"Try and have a little more patience with Dad," said Joyce soberly. "He's changing, Britt. More than he realizes himself. Try and see his point a little. He loved the old ways. He's spent a lifetime at them. And they're hard for him to give up."

They walked apart from the gorge, Joyce leading her horse. Britt could see she had something else on her mind. He waited for her to speak it. Finally she did.

"A little while ago, Britt, you asked me if everything was all right out at Three Link. It isn't."

Larkin flashed her a quick glance. "What isn't, Joyce?"

"You remember the trouble Dad had with a Dutch Klymer, some years back, Britt? Well, Klymer swore then that the day would come when he'd be back on this side of the Royales. Now he is. The word is out that Klymer and nearly a dozen of his men are now headquartering at the Running S. And it has Dad worried."

Larkin knew the story of Dutch Klymer. How at one time, at the head of a number of wilder spirits, Klymer had ridden the high parks of the Royales, living off the beef of other men, slow-elking the same and selling it to the grub shacks of several wildcat mining outfits over on the north side of the Royales. Alec Creager had been the main sufferer at the hands of Klymer and his gang, and had been the main force in running Klymer out of the country. Now Klymer was back, headquartered at the Running S.

"So that's it!" said Larkin. "Now I understand why Jesse Schell has been lying so quiet. He just didn't feel strong enough to tackle us alone, so he's brought in outside help in the shape of Klymer." Larkin paused, frowning in thought. "Wonder what kind of bait Jesse offered Klymer? He wouldn't be here to help Jesse just out of the kindness of his heart. This would be some kind of a strict business deal between the two of them, and for his share, Klymer will be expecting a price."

"That," nodded Joyce, "is exactly how Dad feels. He's wondering if Three Link isn't the price."

Larkin was startled. "Three Link! That couldn't be it, Joyce. Jesse Schell wouldn't stand for that. As little use as I got for Jesse, I can't see him being that low."

The girl shrugged. "What else could Klymer be after? Certainly not you — at least not directly, for you've shipped all your old herd. And Klymer would be after cattle, not range. No, it's Dad that Klymer hates and who he made his threat against, before. As for Jesse Schell, he's headquartering Klymer, isn't he?"

"That makes Jesse an awful dirty scoundrel, Joyce, if you feel that he's made this deal with Klymer at the price of Three Link. Does your father read Jesse that way now?"

"He hasn't said as much right out, but I know what he's thinking. You know, Britt, Dad was really all through with Jesse when he heard of the murder of that squatter, Jed Sharpe. He told Jesse as much. That was what he was telling Jesse the day you and Harley Dodd saw us at the Running S. If you remember, Dad told you not to jump at conclusions, but I think you did."

"Yes, I did," admitted Larkin. "But later I knew better and was sorry. I'm saying so again."

He went into another period of frowning

thought, shaking his head over the implications of all this. "I'm trying to accept the fact that Jesse could creep low enough to sell your father out," he said slowly. "Of course, beyond that I can see that with Klymer's help, Jesse expects to smash me. Which just about puts your father and me and the squatter folks on one side, with Jesse and Klymer on the other. Yes, we're all in it together. I wonder how your father will feel about that, Joyce?"

"Why don't you ride over and find out? You used to know the trail to Three Link."

"Maybe I've been doubtful of my welcome. The last time I was there I hardly heard any trumpets blowing."

Joyce pulled on her buckskin gauntlets, gathered her reins and went swiftly into the saddle. She looked down at Larkin.

"Times change, and so do the minds of people — about many things." Then, as she stirred the sorrel to movement she added, "Tell Rose Calloway I think she's lovely."

Before Larkin could answer she was gone, riding her horse as though she were a part of it. He watched her out of sight, then went back to where Cass Partee was swinging a sledge and Oake Calloway was turning the drill. He gave them the word, then got his horse and rode up into the timber where Len Revis and the Dodd brothers were working with ax and saw.

Here again he told of Dutch Klymer and the implications of Klymer's presence.

"To a certain extent I'm just guessing," he admitted. "Maybe Klymer is still just a small time thief and slow-elker, and he won't be hiding out at Running S very long. But we can't take chances. We got to be sure. So, you can put aside those tools. You've got about enough logs cut, anyhow. From now on, until we know exactly what Klymer and Jesse are up to, you'll be patrolling all the trails. But never alone. Always two and two. Harley and Chuck together and Len, you locate Sod Tremper and the two of you stick together. Don't take anything for granted."

Len Revis laid aside the ax he'd been wielding. "Two things I want to say. First is, that Jesse Schell is snake-belly low down, havin' anything at all to do with Klymer. Second is, I never been so sick of a tool in my life as I was gettin' of that ax. I been yearnin' to hit saddle leather again. Even bad news can have its good side."

Fort Cord lay still and drowsy in the afternoon sunshine. But when Britt Larkin pulled up in front of the store, Castro came to the door, beckoning with an agitated hand. When Larkin clanked up on the porch, Castro spoke hurriedly.

"Get in here and out of sight, Britt. There's a poisonous little snake in town!"

Larkin stared. "Meaning who, Henry? What are you driving at?"

"Meaning Clint Crowder. He's been hanging around town for the past couple days, lapping up liquor in the Guidon and making all kind of tough talk. About you!"

Larkin shrugged. "Hell! I thought it was something real important. Who cares what a feisty little whelp like Crowder says? Me, I got something else to worry about."

Castro caught Larkin by the arm. "You don't understand, boy. Crowder swears he's goin' to gun you on sight. He could be hidin' out at any corner, waiting for you to show. What the devil could have put him after you this way? You think maybe Jesse Schell is siccing him on?"

Larkin shrugged again. "Could be. And I did rough him up a mite out at Running S headquarters one day when he showed a little too much bristle. I knew it wouldn't set well with him, but I never thought it would be enough to start off on a one man feud."

"Well, he's on one, and you better damn well realize it."

"Maybe I will look him up later. But right now I got things to tell you, Henry. That's what I came to town for. You're risking as much as anybody else in this project of ours and got plenty of good judgement. The job itself is moving along fine, but here are some late developments. See what you think."

Larkin told the storekeeper about the Klymer news, told him of what Joyce Creager said of her father's opinion, and his own conclusions. Castro, listening carefully, nodded gravely.

"I think you're guessing right, Britt. There's a

deal between Schell and Klymer. And like you say, the only reasonable bait that could have pulled Klymer back across the mountains is a chance to get back at Alec Creager. And Jesse Schell is going to either turn Klymer loose with his blessing, or he's going to actually help Klymer against Three Link. And what does that make of Jesse Schell!" The storekeeper shook his head, then answered himself. "It makes him the lowest piece of scum ever to hit this country. It makes him lower than Klymer, even."

Castro searched his pockets for a cigar, lit up and puffed furiously. "What are you going to do about it, Britt?"

"I'm going to see Alec Creager, for one thing. If I can make him see that now his cause is my cause and that of the squatter folks, too, why then we can pool our weight and give Schell and Klymer all they're looking for and then some. This could be the place to get Alec's complete backing, which will be all to the good in the future."

Castro grunted a little skeptically. "He's a hardheaded old coot. Be just like him to go proud and say he'll fight his own fight and tell you to fight yours."

"Could be," said Larkin. "But from the way Joyce spoke, the old boy is showing a change of heart on a lot of things. Maybe I can bring him around. I'm going to try, anyhow. You got any other ideas, Henry?"

"Nothing that listens any better than yours.

Except — Clint Crowder. What about him?"

Larkin made an irritated gesture. "Devil take Clint Crowder! Henry, I think you're buildin' a lot out of nothing. Chances are Crowder will take his mad out on the bottle and forget all his big talk."

"Boy," said the storekeeper, "I've lived a mite longer than you. I've seen my share of Crowder's kind. I can tell the difference between whiskey talk, and the real thing. I tell you, Crowder means business. So you slide out of town quiet, and you stay out. You want to see me about anything, send somebody after me. But you stay out of town!"

"What good would that do?" said Larkin. "If, as you say, Crowder is after my skin now, then he'll still be after it, a month from now, six months from now. And I'm not going to prowl around in the weeds, afraid to show my face, just because of a dirty little whelp like Crowder. If he's so damned anxious to see me, then he won't be disappointed." Larkin started for the door.

Castro caught at him in alarm. "Use your head, boy. This thing could end up in gunsmoke. And you're no gunfighter."

Larkin's jaw stole out. "Not by inclination, Henry. But I can use a gun if I have to. I'm going to see just how tall Crowder stands behind his talk!"

Larkin moved out on to the porch. A slow but definite grind of anger was beginning to grow in him. As if he didn't have enough on his mind, this thing had to crop up. He spun up a cigarette and while he did so, made a long, careful survey of town. Never, he decided, had he seen Fort Cord look more drowsy and peaceful. But from what Henry Castro had said, there was a venomous little rider around here somewhere, full of whiskey and gun talk.

Larkin moved out into the street and along it, suddenly aware of a cold, drawn alertness coursing through him. He moved slowly, yet with definite purpose. There was no telling where Crowder might be, what corner he might step around into view.

There was a stir of movement up by the hotel and Larkin's quick glance flicked that way. Then he relaxed a little. It was Bick Pennell, the livery stable owner. Bick, seeing that he'd gained Larkin's attention, came quietly along the street. As he passed Larkin he flicked up his right hand and stabbed a forefinger toward the Guidon. His words were just the softest of murmurs.

"In there, Britt. Don't give him any edge. Good luck!"

"Thanks, Bick."

He cut straight for the Guidon, then, moving at a quickening pace. At the door of the saloon he paused for a moment, loosened the gun in the holster at his hip, then pushed open the swinging portal and stepped through. He let out his breath in a long, soft sigh.

Only two people were present. The bartender and Clint Crowder. Crowder sat at a poker table, facing the door. He was slumped forward across the table, head on his arms, sound asleep. A whiskey bottle and glass stood on the table beside him.

The bartender looked at Larkin, shrugged and turned up hands expressively. And as Larkin moved quietly along in front of the bar the drink dispenser whispered heavily.

"You'd be justified in blowin' him apart, just like he is. After all the talk he's made about what he intended to do to you — !"

Larkin came up to the poker table, cut around behind Crowder. He leaned over and inched Crowder's gun from the holster, then completed his circle of the table, moved up a chair and sat down, facing Crowder. He knew a feeling of complete letdown. It was like getting ready to strike at a hawk, only to end up hitting a fly.

Larkin's cigarette had gone out, so now he scratched a match, freshened his smoke, then leaned over and thrust the end of the match under Crowder's nose.

Crowder stirred, pushed himself up, sneezed violently. He blinked, staring at Larkin with heavy eyes, stupid from whiskey.

"Having sweet dreams, Crowder?" drawled Larkin.

Crowder cursed, and with the word his eyes sharpened, cleared and blazed. He shoved his chair skittering back, lunged to his feet and slapped a clawing hand toward his empty holster.

"Take it easy, Clint," said Larkin. "You're not going anywhere. Now then, what's all this you got against me, all this fire talk?"

Crowder's only answer was another hard spat curse. Then he was whirling away from the poker table and racing for the open end of the bar.

"Watch him, Holly!" rapped Larkin. "Don't let him get behind there!"

The bartender tried, but he was a heavy, slow moving man, and Crowder was too fast for him. Crowder grabbed a bottle off the back bar shelf, aimed a swing at Holly's head. Holly managed to partially deflect it with an upthrown arm. But that heavy, full bottle clipped him a glancing blow across the side of the head and Holly went tumbling back and down, dazed and half stunned. Crowder dived past him, crouched so the bulwark of the bar hid him fully.

Larkin slid out of his chair, gun drawn, moving toward the door. Crowder, he knew, was after the bar gun. There was always a bar gun of some sort . . .

Twin muzzles of a sawed off shotgun came up over the edge of the bar, with Crowder's head and shoulders behind them. As Larkin had gambled he would, Crowder figured that Larkin would still be somewhere close to the poker table and it was toward this spot that he started to lay the shotgun. Instantly he realized his mistake and tried desperately to whip the gun around. The breath of time lost in this mistake of judgement, was Clint Crowder's last mistake.

Britt Larkin's gun belted the echoes and the slug from it cut a faint gouge in the bar top, before crashing into Clint Crowder's chest, heart high.

Crowder's head fell forward and he slid down behind the bar, setting off both barrels of the shotgun with dying fingers. The roaring smash of the weapon shook the room and funneled buckshot chopped a cloud of splinters from the ceiling.

The bartender came crawling on hands and knees around the open end of the bar, crimson dribbling from a cut on the side of his head.

"Loco!" he mumbled thickly. "He went stark loco!"

Chapter VIII

ALLIANCE

DUTCH KLYMER was a big, dark man with heavily jutting black brows which seemed to push his eyes back into his head, where they lay small and glittering. His face was seamed with lines of hard living. He held a cup of coffee cradled in both hands and looked across the top of it at Jesse Schell.

They were seated at the table in the kitchen of the Running S ranchhouse. Late afternoon sunlight slanted in at one window, making a shaft of warm gold in which dust motes danced and floated. Dutch Klymer's voice was as rough and gravelly as his physical appearance.

"The deal's all right, Schell, only you got it backwards. The word that Widdens brought from you was that Alec Creager was ripe to be picked. Well, that's the thing I'm interested in, and that comes first with me. After Creager's taken care of will be time enough to go after your friend Larkin and that flock of squatters. For that matter, you must be going soft, having to yell for help to throw the fear of God into a bunch of damned, sniveling squatters."

"Not as easy as you think," growled Schell. "There's a lot of them and Larkin has sold them some kind of an idea they like. This ain't a flock of lath and tar paper shanty drifters. They got guns and a couple of tough leaders. They'll fight."

Klymer laughed, scoffingly. "That I got to see. Dig down a little and you'll find they're no different than any other of their kind. You ain't roughed them up enough, that's all."

"Wait until you've looked the layout over," said Schell. "Then you'll see what I mean." He hesitated a moment. "How do you figure to go after Creager?"

Klymer's eyes took on an added glitter. "I smash him! I clean him out, right in his own headquarters. Then, when I've fixed him personally, I take his whole damn herd across the Royales."

Jesse Schell stirred in his chair. "Why not just be satisfied with the Three Link herd, Dutch? That would finish him just as surely as if you'd put a bullet in him."

"You crazy?" Klymer's voice rang harshly. "His herd's scattered all over his range. What would Creager be doin' while I rammed here and there to hell an' gone, trying to bunch his herd for driving? He sure wouldn't be standin' by with his hands folded, watchin' me. That was the mistake I made before, nickin' him for eight or ten head here, a dozen there. It gave him the chance to build up his crew until he had too many men and guns for me, and I had to pull out. Gonna be different this time. He don't get the chance to build up his crew. This time I rub him out. Then me and my boys can take our own damn sweet time with the cattle."

While speaking, Klymer had been watching Jesse closely, marking every shade of expression on Jesse's heavy features. Now Klymer leaned forward, fixing Jesse with those little, hard-glittering eyes.

"You ain't goin' to go soft on me, are you, Jesse? You ain't goin' to back away and turn squeamish? You do, and by God, I'll bust you the same as I bust Creager! You asked me to come across the Royales, remember? Now I'm here and I don't stand no foolishness from you or anybody else!"

Jesse couldn't meet the impact of Klymer's eyes. For in them he saw a ruthlessness that was complete and unyielding. He answered with a hurried hoarseness.

"Hell, no, Dutch! I'm going all the way with you."

Klymer pushed back his chair and stood up. "You damn well better, Jesse. I'm goin' to hold you to that. Now I'm takin' a little ride, to scout things a bit. It'll probably be after dark when I get back."

Jesse Schell sat right where he was for a long time after Dutch Klymer had gone. A great uneasiness lay in Jesse. He'd had his good look at the men Klymer had brought in with him, and in them he saw a gang that would stop at nothing. Murder, rapine, fire — nothing! And he, Jesse Schell, had brought them across the mountains.

What about Alec and Joyce Creager? Once they had been his best friends. Once, in his heavy, unimaginative way he had had ideas about Joyce Creager. Every man should have a wife, and who better than Joyce Creager? That was the way Jesse had figured at one time.

But things had changed. Alec and Joyce Creager had changed. Creager had refused to back his hand against the squatters, and Joyce had become as distant as the stars. Both of them looked at him now with a strange new something in their eyes, looks which Jesse couldn't interpret, but which stirred him up and filled him with a blind, thwarted cursing. They looked at him as though he were something far beneath them.

Of course, Britt Larkin had figured in matters, too. Larkin — That damned Britt Larkin — !

Jesse paced up and down the room, ponderous, heavy footed, his face working under the lash of memories. That day Larkin had made him get off the trail — Whipped him off it, by God! Man to man, with Joyce Creager watching. A day, Jesse told himself, that he'd never forget, nor even try to forget until he saw Larkin lying dead in front of him.

That memory had burned at Jesse Schell like some malignant acid. It had ridden him through the day, kept him awake at night. It had taken him into the depths of a whiskey bottle a dozen times, then mocked him through the numbed haze of mind and movement when the bottle was empty. It had obsessed him to the point where it had become like a live coal, seething in his grain.

He slammed a clenched fist into an open palm with a vehemence that left the palm numb. Larkin was the real reason he'd made this deal with Dutch Klymer. Yeah, that was it, Larkin! For Larkin was tied in with the squatters and when he broke the squatters, then he'd have Larkin where he wanted him.

That was half of the deal he'd made with Dutch Klymer, and he had wanted it to be the first half. But Klymer wouldn't go along that way. Klymer had an ax of his own to grind with Alec Creager, and that was the ax Klymer insisted be ground first.

Outside, hoofs rattled up, and then it was Duke Nulk, spurs dragging, who came in. Nulk had been to town. Now he spoke abruptly.

"You're minus a hand, Jesse. Clint Crowder's dead!"

Jesse spun on him. "Dead! How?"

"Larkin. They smoked it out in the Guidon."

Jesse ground his teeth. There it was. Larkin again. Was there no limit to the man's luck?

"How'd it happen?"

Nulk shrugged. "Here's how I got it from

Holly, the bartender." He told it as he had heard it. "Crowder always did figger himself a damn side lot taller than he was. He made a fool play."

"And Larkin wasn't hurt?"

"Nary a scratch," said Nulk. "Me, I hate Larkin's hide and guts as much as any man alive. But I'm tellin' you, Jesse, he ain't a safe man to underestimate. Crowder made that mistake. Don't you."

Jesse pounded his palm again. "I'll get him! He'll be taken care of."

Nulk shrugged again and went out. Jesse resumed his pacing up and down. Clint Crowder, dead. At the hand of Britt Larkin. More salt to rub in a wound already raw. Jesse's thoughts ran savage.

What if Alec Creager did have to be smashed first, before he and Klymer could get at Larkin? After all, what did he really owe Creager? Nothing, not a damn thing. Creager had let him down, hadn't he, refusing to go through with him against the squatters? So why waste any sympathy on Creager? It all came back to that old feeling with Jesse. If a man wasn't for him, he was against him. That was it. So, to hell with Creager!

Jesse stopped in front of a wall cupboard. He jerked it open, took out a whiskey bottle and glass. He poured a heavy slug of liquor and gulped it. He smacked his lips and his heavy face settled into sullen, brutal lines. Yeah, to hell with Alec Creager!

And with that thought, Jesse Schell buried beyond all recovery any shred of conscience he might ever have owned.

Britt Larkin barely beat sunset to the home headquarters. Pale smoke was coiling from the cabin chimney, and by the horses in the corral, he knew that Len Revis and the Dodd brothers were there. Old Sod Tremper was there, too. Len Revis was busy putting together the evening meal.

"Been havin' a little council of war, us four," informed Len, "layin' out the trails to patrol, so we wouldn't be doublin' up. Anything new showed, Britt?"

Larkin dropped down on the edge of one of the wall bunks. "Yeah," he said wearily. "I had to kill Clint Crowder." He stared at the floor, burned out emotion in his look and manner.

They came around as one, all four of them. "Tell us," asked Harley Dodd succinctly.

Larkin told them. He made it brief, colorless, matter-of-fact. But that very brevity of words carried its own impact. Harley cleared his throat.

"The man handling you gave him out at Running S that day must have set him off, Britt."

Len Revis came across, dropped a hand on Larkin's shoulder. "You rubbed out a vicious little whelp, boy. He asked for it."

"That's one for Jed Sharpe," put in Sod Tremper.

They left it that way. Len Revis went back to

his cooking chore, rattling pots and pans. The rest switched to other talk, and gradually some of Larkin's dark mood began to lift. It was good to be within his own four walls, with men who understood his problems and who stood with him in all things. But there was no end to the problems, it seemed, and as they sat down to eat, Larkin brought up the one of Dutch Klymer.

"I've been thinking a lot on that angle," he said. "About Dutch Klymer, I mean. What we don't know is who Klymer and Schell will hit at first, the folks in the valley, us, or Alec Creager. If it's Creager, he'll need help. For Alec's not as young as he used to be and while he's got some damn good men in his crew, there's not enough of them. Anybody got any ideas?"

"Yeah," said Len Revis, "I have. I'm not tryin' to tell you what to do, Britt. But I do say we'd be the biggest sort of fools to sit back dumb and blind and let Schell and Klymer call their shots. Whichever way they hit, it's reasonable to figger they'll be aimin' for surprise. Me, I figger it would help our side plenty if we could turn that surprise right back in their faces. So, instead of wastin' too much time along the trails, I think we ought to have a man keepin' an eye on Running S headquarters all the time, Britt. Day and night. Then we'll know the minute Schell and Klymer start to move, and in what direction. Mebbe that way we can have a lot more waiting for them when they arrive than what they figger on."

"Good head, Len," said Larkin. "We'll do it. Only, not just one man watching them, but two. That way, one man can bring the word and the other can still watch them in case they feint one way and go another. I'm not giving Schell too much credit for foxiness, but I am Klymer. So we'll forget about patrolling trails. You boys stand shift, two and two, starting tonight. Fix it up among yourselves as to the shifts."

"Me," said Sod Tremper, "I allus did get along pretty well under the stars. What say, Len?"

"With you," answered Len. He turned to Chuck Dodd. "Come dawn tomorrow, Sod an' me'll see you and Harley up on that big timber point above Running S. Fair enough?"

"We'll be there," nodded Chuck.

Dusk came in, blue and still. Len and Sod Tremper caught and saddled and rode away. Larkin put on his hat and leather jacket.

"I'm riding down for a talk with Oake Calloway and Cass Partee," he told Chuck and Harley. "Tomorrow I go see Alec Creager. We got to organize for this thing. Might be wise for you boys to throw your blankets back in the edge of the timber. No telling what kind of ideas Klymer and Schell are cooking up."

Up on a fresh horse, Larkin dropped down the mountain slope in night's first full dark. He thought of the night he and Len had ridden this way and of their meeting with Jesse Schell and his down-charging outfit. A lot of things had happened since then.

He left the timber and broke into the full starlight of the open valley. Here a little wind was stirring, going nowhere in particular. But it had a spice of distance in it that was good in a man's lungs, and Larkin put his face to it with a keen edge of pleasure.

Camp fires twinkled on the flats and there were larger areas of glow where the uprooted and piled up sage of the day had burned down to ruby coals. Larkin knew a grim satisfaction when a voice challenged from the shadows. Cass Partee had his guards out.

"Name yourself!"

"Larkin."

"Come in."

There was an air of quiet satisfaction about the squatter camp. Men and women who had labored fully throughout the day, now were drawing on the restful peace and ease of night. They held their little family groups about the fires, some content with silence, others trading quiet talk. Some of the kids skylarked about and over by one fire a banjo plunked and twanged softly.

Larkin located the Calloway fire, where he found Oake and Rose and Cass Partee. Rose was tending a simmering pot on the fire and the men were lounging and smoking.

"Last of the fresh beef in that pot, Britt," greeted Oake Calloway. "Do we dare ask for more?"

"Of course. When the critters I saved out of

my herd are gone, we'll make a deal with Alec Creager for some of his."

Larkin dropped on his heels and built a cigarette. The firelight picked out his features in bold bronze. It was a face that had known changes in the past couple of months. The old, easy, relaxed humor was gone, replaced by a certain hardness and a settled gravity. The jaw angles had sharpened there was grimness about the eyes and lips. Larkin felt these three people watching him and his head came up.

"Work going all right?"

Cass Partee nodded quickly. "Couldn't be better." His glance dropped to the gun at Larkin's hip. "We're all mighty glad you're good with that."

"Crowder?"

Cass nodded again. "Jim Dykes went to town. He brought back the word. We feel somehow responsible. If it wasn't for us showing here in this valley, you wouldn't have had men like Crowder after you."

Larkin shrugged. "No fault of yours in any way." Then he added soberly, "There's going to be more like it, I'm afraid. A man just has to realize that nothing worth while in this life comes easy."

"You're driving at something," said Oake Calloway. "What is it?"

"I gave you some word about this Dutch Klymer hombre already," Larkin said. "Since then I been sounding out opinion. The signs all point just one way. A tie in between Klymer and Jesse Schell for a big push to smash you, me, and Alec Creager. It figures up that Jesse Schell aims to sell out Alec Creager, a man who's been his best friend."

Larkin paused, drew a final inhale on his cigarette, spun the butt into the fire. "Alec Creager," he went on, "is a good man. Oh, sure, he was a little scratchy about you folks at first, but he's coming around, I think. He's no longer young and his crew isn't too big, not near big enough to stand up to what Schell and Klymer can throw at him. So, now we come to the point." He looked straight at Oake Calloway. "Would you folks be willing to back Creager's hand in a showdown?"

Oake had been nursing a corn cob pipe. Now he thrust a twig into the fire, set it ablaze, then brushed the flame back and forth across the pipe bowl, while his cheeks curved inward as he puffed.

"You're going to back Creager?"

"Of course. All the way."

"Then," said Calloway solidly, "we'll back him. As I see it, there's just two sides to this thing, with no halfway angles. One side is where Jesse Schell stands. The other side is all the rest of us. Yeah, we'll back Creager." Then he added, with a grim smile, "That could change Creager's opinion of squatters."

"What you got in mind for us, Britt?" asked Cass Partee.

"Any of you people got saddles?"

"Just two that I know of. I got an old one and Jim Dykes has one."

"I can rake up four more from Bick Pennell in town," Larkin said. "I'll bring down half a dozen saddle broncs from my cavvy. You pick six of your younger men who can ride a little, and shoot a lot, if they have to. Have them keep the horses handy at all times, so they can move out at a minute's notice. With six of you, me and my crew, and the Three Link crew, we'll have enough men to give Schell and Klymer all the argument they want. That will still leave enough older men among you to keep an eye on things down this way."

Rose Calloway, listening quietly, had come around the fire to sit beside Cass Partee. Now Larkin saw her hand steal out and settle over one of Partee's.

"This sort of thing is tough on you women, Rose," Larkin said. "Believe me, I wouldn't ask it if I didn't feel it was necessary. I'll do my best not to lead anyone into an angle too tight to get out of."

The firelight showed the serene, strong beauty in her face. Her glance was steady and level as she looked at Larkin. "Facts are made to be faced, Britt. On one side there is Jesse Schell and this Dutch Klymer. On the other side are all the rest of us. All of us!"

Larkin looked at her admiringly. "Jesse Schell has made a lot of mistakes. His biggest one was thinking you folks would scare." He straightened up. "Pick your men, Cass. Talk it over with them. Make them understand that it won't be a soft ride, that it could be a pretty rough one. I'll have the horses and the other saddles here tomorrow."

Heading out for home again, Larkin suddenly knew the weight of weariness. It wasn't so much a physical thing as it was mental. For there was a vast sense of responsibility riding on him. Many men were now regarding him as a leader, believing in him, trusting his judgement. Men ready to follow him into the fog of gunsmoke. A mistake in judgement on his part could leave good men lying dead in the dust, could mean the shattered dreams and hopes of good women. It wasn't easy realization to ride with.

And then that affair in town with Crowder. A thing that drained a man of something. Even though thoroughly justified, it still left its dark shadow. Then there was the uncertainty of the future. Which way would Jesse Schell and Dutch Klymer jump, and when?

He shook his head, pushing the dark thoughts aside. He set his face to the night wind coming down off the Royales, breathed deep of its wild goodness. Tomorrow was another day.

An hour after sunup the next morning, Larkin crossed the line where his and the Three Link range joined. There he met up with Stony Cuff, a Three Link rider, who had just turned back a small bunch of Three Link cattle. Stony grinned and begged a smoke.

"Never was over fond of fences," he said. "But I could wish there was one along this range line."

Larkin handed over his sack of Durham. "Keep it, Stony. Got more in my saddle bags. Now, what's all this fence talk?"

"Alec's had us scratchin' gravel, driftin' cattle over this side of headquarters," explained Stony. "And, cow nature being what it is, a lot of the pesky brutes keep tryin' to move over on to your grass, and they're keepin' me in a sweat turnin' 'em back."

"Why bother to turn 'em back?" said Larkin. "Let 'em go. I won't be needing any of this grass until next spring. I got plenty of grass further back for what cattle I'll have until then. Hell, man, let them go, and welcome."

"Sounds good to me," Stony said. "But I can't do it without orders from Alec. He was plenty definite about holdin' the cattle at this line."

"What's Creager's idea of stripping his west range? Grass all used up?"

Stony shook his head. "Not a question of grass so much as it is of neighbors," was his dry remark. "Runnin' S ain't as popular with us as it used to be. What with Dutch Klymer movin' in with Jesse Schell, Alec figgers we better keep temptation as far away from Runnin' S as possible. Klymer, y'know, allus did fancy the other feller's cows. Say, what's this talk I hear about you and Clint Crowder?"

Larkin shrugged soberly. "True. Something I didn't enjoy. But he would have it."

"So I heard. Wouldn't waste any sleep over it, was I you, Britt. Crowder allus did fancy himself that way. His mistake. Doggone it, there's another bunch of critters tryin' to pull a sneak on me."

Stony spurred away, cutting across the long, open park.

The closer he got to Three Link, the more cattle Larkin saw. Creager was certainly moving everything east of headquarters. Which told something. It told of a change in Creager and his thinking, of caution and a desire to avoid trouble, even at the cost of pride. The Alec Creager of a few years ago wouldn't have moved a single head, just because such as Dutch Klymer had shown up on the range. He'd have spit in Klymer's eye and dared him to do his damndest.

Riding in to Three Link, Larkin saw Alec Creager helping Tom Adin hook a team up to the ranch spring wagon. Adin was his usual enigmatic, still-faced self, but his eyes were friendly. Frosty-browed old Alec looked grim and a little tired and worried. He showed Larkin a gruff nod.

"Any objection to me running a couple of wires across the most open parks along the line of our ranges? Temporary, of course. But right now it's keepin' us jumping to hold our cattle on our side of the line. A couple of wires, strung in the right places, would help a lot."

"No need of wire or line riding either," answered Larkin. "Let your cows go, Alec. I won't be needing that grass for a while and you're welcome to it until then."

Creager gave him a swift, direct look. "That's damn generous."

Tom Adin murmured softly, "See, Alec — I told you."

Creager flushed. "I'll pay grazing rights, of course."

"No," said Larkin. "You won't pay me for anything. But here's what you can do. You can sell me an occasional beef to keep the cooking pots full, down in the valley. Those people are working hard and need fresh beef. I've saved some of my own critters for that purpose, but I can see now that I didn't keep out enough."

Creager spoke slowly. "Joyce was telling me of the job you got the squatters working at. I got to admit that maybe you got a pretty sound idea there. Now I never thought I'd live to see the day when I could stand the thought of Three Link beef filling the bellies of a flock of squatters without me bursting an artery. But," and here he smiled grimly, "a man can change his mind, I guess. Anyhow, take what you want when you want it, and this time I'm the one to say no payment. Tom, you see to it that our boys get that word."

"Now," drawled Adin, "we're at last comin' down to cases and common sense."

Larkin spun up a smoke. "What about that new partnership over west, Alec?"

Creager's face drew into a case of bitterness. "I'll wait that one out. It may mean nothing, it may mean plenty. What do you think?"

"I'll give you the word of Oake Calloway. As he sees it, it's Jesse Schell and Dutch Klymer on one side, and all the rest of us on the other."

"Shrewd hombre, Calloway," put in Tom Adin.

Alec Creager stared into the distance, considering. There was still some of the old stubbornness in him, but it was obviously breaking up.

"I thought better of Jesse than that, taking up with a damned known cow thief," he admitted finally. "I'm not sure I can see what he expects to gain by it."

"Look at it from this angle, Alec," said Larkin. "He came to realize that you weren't going to back his hand against the squatters, and through them, against me. That left him on his own, and not strong enough to tackle us alone. So he sends outside for help, for Dutch Klymer. But common sense suggests that Klymer didn't come in across the mountains to help Jesse just for the hell of it. They've made a deal of some sort. Klymer swore he'd get even with you some day, didn't he? Well — ?"

Alec Creager made a hard gesture with a cutting right hand. "Damn it, man, you're saying that Jesse has agreed to side in with Klymer against me, if Klymer will back his hand against you and the squatters. I can't believe Jesse would do that. Why, we've been friends and neighbors for years."

"You got a better answer, Alec?" queried Larkin dryly. "Klymer's headquartering at the Running S, isn't he? You sure wouldn't have him around your place, and I wouldn't have him around mine. Yet Jesse has taken him in with open arms."

"Right!" said Tom Adin. "Might as well face facts, Alec."

The Three Link foreman turned and began unhooking the spring wagon team. Joyce Creager came out of the ranchhouse and crossed over to them, drawing on her gauntlets.

"Hello, Britt," she greeted quietly. She turned to her father. "I thought we were driving to town for a load of barbed wire?"

"No need of it now," Creager told her. "Larkin says it's all right if some of our cattle cross over on to his grass."

Joyce flashed Larkin a quick glance, then spoke slowly. "Someday I hope we can start in giving, instead of always taking."

"Your father is now, Joyce," said Larkin. "He's going to give some beef to the folks down in the valley."

"Really, Dad?"

Creager nodded. "That's right."

"Now I can ride with my head up again," Joyce said. She caught her father's arm and squeezed it. "Tom, would you catch up my sorrel for me?

I'm still going to town. There's the mail and a couple of other errands I want to do."

She followed Adin over to the corrals. Alec Creager, watching her, spoke with rueful gruffness. "She's been givin' me fits, saying I'd eventually benefit by the job you and the squatters are doing, Britt. And that I should be helping. So, if it's not too late, and if you're needin' money, I'd like to kick in with my share."

Larkin ground his cigarette butt under his heel, a smile breaking across his face. He put out his hand.

"Shake, Alec. This is what I've been waiting and hoping for. Not your money, exactly, though I may have to hold you to that. The big thing is knowing that you're willing to back the deal. This will give those people down in the flats a real lift. We need you with us. Yeah, this is a big day."

"Kinda feel that maybe it is, myself," admitted Creager. "Now, what are we goin' to do about Jesse Schell and Dutch Klymer?"

The smile faded from Larkin's face. "Watch 'em, Alec. I got men doing that, right now. A day and night watch on Running S. When and if Schell and Klymer make a crooked move, we hit them, all out! You, me and the squatters. The folks on the flats have agreed to that. Things have come to just such a pass. We'd be fools not to recognize it, Alec."

Alec Creager pushed a hand across his forehead. "I'd hoped," he said slowly, "to ride the rest of the trail in peace. When a man grows old, the fighting fire in him burns dimmer, Britt. Mostly, all he asks is to be left alone. But," and here his head went back and a glint of the old flame showed in his deep set eyes, "if fight he must, fight he will, by God! You got anything to suggest?"

"Yeah," nodded Larkin. "Don't worry too much about your cattle. Don't scatter your men. Keep them pretty close to headquarters. Keep somebody on watch by day, and a couple of guards out by night. Like I said, I got men watching Running S. Should Klymer start fooling around your cattle, you'll get word. Plenty of time then to do something about it. But I got a feeling that Klymer has rougher ideas than that."

"Like a try at hitting me right here at headquarters?"

"It's a possibility not to be overlooked," Larkin said. "Go ahead and wait this thing out. But be set against a surprise. The folks in the valley are organized that way. When Jesse and Klymer do make their move, maybe they'll be the ones to be surprised."

Creager considered for a moment, then slowly nodded. "Make's sense. I'll do it that way." He bent a very direct look on Larkin. "Hear you run into a rough spot in town."

"Clint Crowder?"

"That's right."

Larkin spoke gravely. "Why must some push

things that far? Now I feel like I got a stain on me. People look at me and I wonder what they're thinking."

Creager dropped a hand on Larkin's shoulder. "If they're the right kind, they won't blame you. And if they're the other kind, then it doesn't matter a damn what they think." Joyce came riding over from the corrals. Larkin moved toward his own horse. "I was figuring on town myself after I left here, Joyce. If you don't mind, I'll jog along with you."

Tom Adin and Alec Creager watched them ride away. "Tom," said Creager abruptly, "it comes to me that mebbe I've misjudged Britt Larkin."

"You have," agreed Adin with pointed quietness. "But as long as you've come to realize it, I guess there's no great harm done. You and Britt had your heads together pretty sober. Decide on something?"

Creager told him what Larkin had said. "I still find it hard to believe Jesse Schell would be partner to anything quite as rough and treacherous as that. Yet, I'd be a fool to overlook the possibility. So, you go gather in Stony and Race and Cotton. We'll stick close to headquarters and we'll watch and wait. It's as good a plan as any."

Creager went back to the ranchhouse. Tom Adin finished unhooking and unharnessing the spring wagon team and turned them back into the corral. Then he caught up a saddle mount, cinched his kak in place. But before he left he went over to the bunkhouse and came back with a scabbarded Winchester rifle. He slung this to his saddle, under the near stirrup leather, then swung up and headed out.

As he rode, Tom Adin pulled the Winchester from its saddle boot, cracked the action to make certain it was loaded, then slid it back into the leather again. He lifted his horse to a jog.

Chapter IX

TIME AND TENSION

JOYCE CREAGER rode for a considerable distance in silence. Jogging along beside her through the nodding timber, Britt Larkin knew a certain quiet contentment he'd been missing for a long time. This, he thought, was like it had been in the old days. Joyce and he, drifting through the scented shadows, with no pressure of disagreement between them. A chance to watch her, straight and sure in the saddle, a shaft of dappled sunlight striking her now and then, touching her cheeks with warm color, putting a shine on her head. Feeling his glance, Joyce stirred and finally spoke.

"Strange how things work out, isn't it? That last time we were completely alone on this trail, I was doing my best to hit you with my quirt. And you, you — !" She stopped, flushing.

"I had that quirting coming, Joyce," Larkin said quickly. "I was wrong in a lot of ways that day, things I said, what I did."

"Not so wrong in what you said," she challenged. "You hit too close to the truth for comfort. I have been spoiled to death. I have been pretty useless. Selfish, too, I think. Living safe and secure in my own little world, with never a thought of how rough life might be for others less fortunate. You — you were comparing me with some of those squatter women, weren't you?"

Larkin squirmed in his saddle. "I want you to know I've taken it all back."

"You shouldn't," she said evenly. "For it's done me a lot of good. It was one of the best things that ever happened to me. Oh, it made me furiously angry at the time, but that was because I was hearing the real truth about myself for the first time. Later, when I had cooled off enough to think about it clearly, I had to admit that. I've been trying to change. I think I've made some progress." She showed him a small, crooked smile. "What do you think?"

He smiled back at her. "I think you've made a howling liar out of me."

She rode again for some time in silence, the smile still lingering on her expressive lips. Then she sobered and spoke abruptly of something else.

"That affair with Clint Crowder must have been pretty terrible."

Larkin was slow in answering. "It wasn't pretty," he admitted finally. "I'm no way proud of it."

She flashed a quick look at him. He was staring

straight ahead, his face carved in a sort of grave stillness. "Dad told me about it," she said. "He said you did only what you had to do, that there was no other way out. You've changed his ideas on a lot of things, Britt, including yourself."

Larkin seized on the change of subject, relaxing a little. "From what he told me, you've been currying him some. Helping to change those ideas."

They moved out of the timber into the open sunshine of the valley slope. Down on the flats the same heavy columns of smoke from burning sage were rolling up. East along the lower slope a haze of amber dust lifted, where men were at work with the Fresno scrapers. The dull, hard echoes of a blast came rolling out of the distant river gorge. Joyce's eyes glistened as she looked and listened.

"Would you understand what I mean, Britt, when I say that all that makes me feel good inside?"

Larkin nodded quickly. "Sure I would. I feel the same way. It means we're going some place instead of just stomping up and down in the same place for the rest of our days."

They hit the valley floor and went along the dusty way between tall mats of sage that were still uncleared. Larkin was pleasurably surprised at the change in this girl beside him. For now she rode almost gaily, singing a little soft song to herself.

"Yeah," he drawled. "Things change and so do people. Like you. All of a sudden you're as full of life as a cricket. Why?"

She looked at him with a faintly jeering smile. "Well, it is a nice day, isn't it?"

He shook his head. "Len Revis says all women are uncertain critters. He's right."

She laughed and let him wonder.

Fort Cord lifted out of the heat haze ahead, and so did a banner of approaching dust. A twist in the trail showed four riders approaching. Even at a distance there was no mistaking the hulking figure of Jesse Schell as one of them.

Joyce's mood of gaiety left her instantly. Larkin saw the change in his companion and understood the reason.

"Steady," he said quietly. "Nothing to worry about." He swung his horse closer to her, leaving half the trail open.

Though he had spoken words of comfort to Joyce, he didn't blind himself to possibilities. He fixed the approaching group with a fine alertness, dropping his hand to his side, close to the butt of the gun which hung there.

As the distance narrowed, Larkin put his attention on the man riding at Jesse Schell's side. A big, dark-faced man, with heavy brows and little, cold eyes. Larkin had heard plenty about Dutch Klymer, but had never seen the man before. Yet he knew instantly that this was Klymer. The two riding behind Schell and Klymer were strangers to him, but they had all the ear-marks of their trade.

A flush grew and darkened in Jesse Schell's heavy face. He instinctively started to lift a hand toward his hat as his eyes touched Joyce Creager, but the gesture stopped half completed. And under the proud directness of Joyce's glance, Jesse's eyes slid away.

Not so with the man beside him. Dutch Klymer's glance ran up and down Joyce's slender grace with a crass boldness that sent a quick rage coursing through Larkin, and he knew the quick urge to drag his gun and smash Klymer across the face with it. But common sense whispered in time and Larkin kept the seething boil of feeling from showing on the surface. His face was a still, inscrutable mask as they came even with the group and passed them.

Larkin knew an almost uncontrollable impulse to look back. The broad area between his shoulders tightened. How did he know that a slug wouldn't come hammering into him? For they were the kind of men who might pull such a deal. . . .

But the distance between them increased and the muffled tempo of hoofs faded out. Larkin let out a breath he hadn't realized he'd been holding. To his companion he kept his tone light.

"See? I told you there was nothing to worry about."

"I — I'm shaking all over," stammered Joyce. "That — that man with Jesse. The dark one. Did you notice his eyes, Britt? Did you ever see anything more evil?"

"Dutch Klymer," said Larkin. "He keeps on hanging around this range he'll get that look taken out of him. But they're long gone now, so cheer up and start singing again. I like you that way."

Slowly the color came back into Joyce's face. But she rode the rest of the way into Fort Cord in silence. As they pulled up and dismounted in front of Henry Castro's store, Joyce flashed another look at the man beside her. There was a mysterious softness in her eyes.

Up in the high parks, Tom Adin was riding. He'd already sought out Stony Cuff and given him word to head back to headquarters. Now Tom was heading east to locate Race Wallace and Cotton Barr.

All the parks were full of Three Link cattle, a fact Adin noted with satisfaction. Moving the bulk of the Three Link herd over this way was a common sense move, considering present conditions; the further the cattle could be moved from the limits of Running S range, the better.

With his practiced cattleman's eye, Adin noted the stock were in good condition. Come fall and shipping time, they'd be good and fat. But Tom Adin had seen more than one shipping herd, sleek and fat when leaving the Royales, drain off a lot of that fat on the long, barren drag to the railroad yards at Button Willow. So, he was able to fully appreciate the sound motives behind Britt Larkin's plan for feed stations at the watering spots along the way.

In his quiet manner, Adin had been hinting his approval of Larkin's scheme right along to Alec Creager. He knew Creager too well to try and force the crusty old timer and had relied on time and conditions to bring Creager around. Now these factors were working and Creager had supplied his nod of approval. Over this, Tom Adin felt real satisfaction.

He left one park, traveled a shadowy way through a spread of timber and then broke into another open area. Here he pulled up abruptly. There were cattle in this park. There were also three riders, grouped over near the upper edge of it. They were sitting their saddles quietly, watching the cattle and having some kind of discussion among themselves. They were strangers to Adin and now they straightened in their saddles and watched him.

Tom Adin was neither coward nor foolhardy. Had he discovered these three before showing himself, he'd have kept to the timber and watched them from that shelter. But he was in the open now and they had seen him. And their interest in Three Link cattle was just a little too pointed to be passed up. So Adin rode over toward them.

They held their ground, though they did spread out a little. Coming up to face them, Adin saw that they were all armed and, after a pointed, direct survey, he decided he didn't like their looks.

"Looking for something, maybe?" he asked bluntly.

"Maybe," was the insolent retort of one of them. "Concern of yours?"

"I'm making it so." Adin jerked his head toward the cattle scattered across the park. "They belong to Alec Creager, if you didn't know. Getting ideas about them?"

"And if we were?"

"Mistake on your part," shot back Adin. "Bad mistake. I suggest you drift."

"Proud hombre, ain't he?" drawled another of the three. "What about, I wonder? Mebbe he thinks he owns the world. Might be fun to show him otherwise."

The speaker had a hatchet face, with a thin, straggly beard. He sat leaning a little forward in his saddle, watching Tom Adin with eyes as hard as those of a hunting hawk. This fellow had an idea that he plainly relished, and now he voiced it.

"Yeah, we'll show him. He'll do the driftin', not us. You hear that, fellah? You do the driftin', not us. You turn around and get outa here. But before you go, we'll just take over those guns of yours. Ain't nothin' that cuts the comb of a proud rooster like takin' his guns off him. Brings him right down to size. Rufe, get over there and lift his weapons!"

Tom Adin realized he'd ridden into something. But he wasn't giving up his guns to any three like these. He settled himself in the saddle, ready for anything.

"It'll be rough if you want it that way," he said quietly.

"First he got proud, now he'd get tough," mocked the one with the beard. "Fancies himself, for a fact. We'll see. Rufe, you heard what I said, didn't you? Go gather his guns!"

Rufe started, then stopped abruptly as a voice hit out harshly from the edge of a jackpine thicket, directly behind the three.

"No, Rufe, don't you try and go anywhere! You just stay damn well put. Rest of you buckos be careful. Damn careful!"

It was Len Revis who stepped from the jackpines. He held a rifle, and it was cocked and ready, half way to his shoulder. The three strange riders jerked their heads around, stiffened into immobility at what they saw. Len grinned like a sardonic old wolf.

"Now ain't it amazin' the way conditions can change? One minute you figger you're a high ace. Next minute you find out you ain't. What was all that about cuttin' the comb of a proud rooster by takin' his guns away? Quite an idea. Oughta work on three turkey buzzards, too. We'll try it. Tom, you drift around and lift the hardware off these funny ones. And if they get too funny they'll wake up in hell, wonderin' what hit 'em!"

The shadow of a smile touched Tom Adin's

lips. "Len, you old scoundrel, you're in a class by yourself."

Adin sent his horse ahead, drifting up beside each of the three in turn, always careful that he didn't get in line between them and that rifle of Len's. One after another he disarmed them, of both their belt guns, and of the rifles they carried in their saddle boots. He tossed the weapons down into the grass.

"I guess that does it, Len. What do you think they're going to do now?"

Len grinned. "I calc'late they're goin' to drift, that way." He jerked the muzzle of his rifle toward the east. "Shag it, you buckos, shag it! And next time don't take so much for granted."

They didn't answer, they didn't argue. They swung their horses and headed east.

Len watched them out of sight, then lowered the hammer of his rifle, dropped down on his heels and built a cigarette. "Some of the gang Dutch Klymer brought in with him, I reckon."

Tom Adin nodded. "Probably. I'm wondering how you happened to show up so handy like?"

Len chuckled. "Been trailin' them fellers ever since they left Runnin' S headquarters early this mornin'. Didn't figger them to be up to too much mischief, but decided I'd tail 'em, just for the hell of it. Sod Tremper and me, we been watchin' Runnin' S all last night. Them three fellers struck out just as the Dodd boys come along to spell Sod and me. Sod, he wanted to trail along with me, but I told him he'd better get along back to Tin Cup and get himself some sleep. He ain't as young as he used to be."

Tom Adin laughed softly. "And you, I suppose, are still in the first bloom of youth?"

"Hum," grunted Len. "Not exactly. But I'm a curious old fool, and I just can't bear not to see what's goin' on. It was worth while, at that. Them looked like pretty good guns you shucked off them jiggers. Might come in handy for the squatter folks. Reckon I'll just take 'em along with me."

"Where's your horse?" Adin asked.

Len jerked his head. "Back yonder in the timber."

A few moments later, his arms full of guns, old Len prowled away.

Work went on at an increasing tempo around the river flats, up in the gorge and across the slope where the Fresno scrapers gouged and slashed. Always close at hand to the sweating, grimy faced toilers were rifles, loaded and ready for any emergency. And whenever men straightened their backs, resting for a moment, they searched all distances with intent eyes. At night, on the flats, the squatter camp was compact and men guarded it in shifts the night through.

Hitched in a row to the feed rack on one side of a big squatter wagon were six good saddle broncs from Britt Larkin's cavvy. On the tongue of the wagon were racked six saddles. Larkin had seen to the horses and saddles and Cass Partee had picked five good men besides himself to saddle and ride any time the occasion called for it.

Larkin himself was again at work with Cass Partee and Oake Calloway, up in the gorge. It was muscle stretching, back breaking work, but gradually the lateral cut through the backbone of rock grew in length, grew until only a wedge of some three feet remained between the waters to come and the head of the gulch which wound down the slope to meet the end of the main ditch which the Fresno scraper crews had fashioned.

Next came the dam, heart of the entire operation. Oake Calloway, doubled hands on hips, stood staring up and across at a rock face on the east side of the gorge.

"Been thinkin' about that pile of stuff up there, Britt. We're going to need weight and plenty of it to anchor the dam logs. That means rock, a lot of it. Now, if we drill enough shot holes and drill 'em in the right places in that face, we can bring the whole cussed thing down. It'll pile up pretty much across the river and, while a lot of smashed up small stuff will wash away, the big pieces will stay put. That'll give us somethin' to build on with our logs. Be a tough chore, but I think it can be done. What say?"

Larkin shrugged. "You know powder, you know rock. Whatever you say goes, Oake."

So they went at it again, with hammer and drill. In some places where they managed footing, they worked with fair ease. But in others they had to be lowered in rope slings from the top of the rock face and then the work was slow and killing, for each shot hole was a one man job, turning a drill with one hand, swinging a short hammer with the other.

The sun burned them and browned them and turned them almost black. The rough surface of the rock scraped and gouged skin from them. Drills went back and forth to Hack Dinwiddie's blacksmith shop in town to be sharpened and resharpened. Finally Hack brought his portable forge and spare anvil out to the spot and labored steadily, the chime of hammer on anvil beating out its own song of echoes.

In between the times when he was sharpening drills, big, slow moving Hack took his turn at drilling shot holes. The first time he showed at this, Larkin went over to him.

"Don't know when I'll be able to scrape up the money to pay you, Hack."

Hack grunted. "Who in hell said anything about pay? If you can stake everything you got on this deal, if these squatter folks can do the same and if Henry Castro can put what he's got on the line, then I don't see why I can't put my weight behind it, too. Gimme room to swing a hammer and I'll show you how to sink a drill into this damn rock." Then, as he saw that Larkin was framing words of thanks, Hack grinned. "Go long with you. Can't you see I'm busy?"

So they went along, fighting the stubborn

rock, and there finally came a day when Oake Calloway judged that all was ready. Powder was packed into shot holes, fuses were cut and capped and put in place. Fuse lengths had to be judged carefully, for as nearly as possible, Oake wanted the effect to be one great shot.

Men and women gathered at a safe distance to watch. At a word, Larkin and Partee and Calloway lit fuses, then scurried to safety. Smoke from the burning fuses curled and writhed in white, spitting spirals. Then it came.

Queerly muffled at first, then breaking out into a ragged, rumbling, splitting roar, which sent tumultuous echoes rolling and bellowing up and down Reservation Valley and along the mountain slope. Rock dust spurted, thickened into a boiling cloud, and tons of split and shattered rock cascaded down into the river, beating the water to a dirty foam. Smaller chunks arched and whizzed through the air like a volley of cannon balls.

When the dust and smoke cleared there was a vast, raw scar on the wall of the gorge and for two thirds its width the river water foamed and fought at a new barrier. Staring at the results, Oake Calloway exulted in two words.

"It worked!"

Men labored waist and shoulder deep in chill mountain water, planting logs in this foundation of shattered rock, logs which Len Revis and the Dodd brothers had cut from the timber groves higher up. Men slipped and floundered and fought that ever pressing water. But they planted those timbers and chained them in place. They pried boulders and jagged rock chunks into greater interlocking security.

They slung bigger chains across the entire length of the dam and anchored the ends of the chain in solid rock. Britt Larkin and Cass Partee made a hurried wagon trip to town and ransacked Bick Pennell's livery barn storeroom and loft for every empty oat sack they could find. These were filled with sand and gravel and placed where they would do the most good.

Less and less water found freedom past the dam. And down below, at the falls, the heavy pound of tumbling water gradually diminished. Above the dam a pond formed, each day stretching a little further up stream, each day lipping higher until finally it began working back into the lateral cut, filling this.

The days slid by, lost in toil and purpose. Britt Larkin was living wholly at the squatter camp now. He'd brought down a roll of blankets from the ranch, which he'd spread near one of the wagons. He ate his meals with Cass Partee and the Calloways and he crawled into his blankets each night to sleep like a dead man.

A growing excitement was taking hold of the camp. The ditching to the flats was about completed, the dam was holding. Water filled the lateral cut. There remained only the building of a sluice gate to control the flow of water and then a final blast at the outer end of the lateral to clear the final thin barrier. The dream which had seemed so distant at one time, was now almost an actuality.

To Britt Larkin, Oake Calloway said, "We can't expect everything to be a finished job. I'm sure the heart of the dam will hold against winter and spring freshets and by then we'll have made it so solid and lasting, nothing can move it. The ditching will have to be improved, too, but we can't do it all in just a few weeks or months. All I want is to see water on these flats, once! Then I'll know it can be put there forever."

This night, in his blankets, Larkin knew a restlessness that he couldn't account for. Maybe it was because there were so many people he'd seen nothing of these past few weeks. Like Joyce and Alec Creager. What about them? How were things at Three Link?

And what about Jesse Schell and Dutch Klymer? When would they ride? Things had been going along almost too quietly. There was something almost ominous in this false peace that had fallen. Yet, Larkin knew that Len Revis and the Dodd brothers and old Sod Tremper were standing watch, up there in the Royales. So long as they brought no alarm, then all must be well. With this comforting thought, he fell asleep.

It was only a little later that he awoke. He got the message through the earth he slept on, the thud of distant hoofs, hurrying hoofs, coming steadily closer. He pushed up on one elbow and listened. He heard a guard call a challenge, heard Harley Dodd answer. Larkin was instantly out of his blankets, pulling on his boots. He went out to meet Harley and Harley gave him the word.

"They're ridin' tonight, Britt! Jesse Schell and Dutch Klymer. Len Revis brought the word. Him and Sod Tremper relieved Chuck and me just after sunset. Chuck and me were back at headquarters, just finishin' supper when Len came in with the word. He said Schell and Klymer had pulled out in full force, that they'd split up, Schell ridin' high, Klymer cuttin' down lower. Len said to tell you it looked like they were figgerin' on hittin' from above and below at the same time."

"Three Link?" Larkin's words were bleak.

"That's right. Alec Creager is in for it!"

Chapter X

CRIMSON NIGHT

CASS PARTEE and Oake Calloway had come up. Larkin turned to them.

"You heard?"

"We heard," said Cass. "Whatever you say, Britt. We're with you."

Larkin rolled a cigarette while he considered. He couldn't make a mistake in this. The consequences could be too disastrous. He spoke slowly.

"It could be a feint. They could have found out some way that we've been watching them, and in this move aim to pull us one way while they intend to hit from another. Maybe make a move toward Three Link but instead hit this camp."

"They do," growled Calloway, "we'll be waiting for them. Don't let any worry about this camp tie your hands, Britt."

"Then we'll play it like it looks," said Larkin. "Three Link. Cass, get your men and saddle up. I'll ride with you. Harley, you skin on back and pick up Chuck and Len and Sod. Ride high. Get clear above Schell. Then, if it is Three Link they're after, we'll give them just what they're planning for Creager. We'll hit them from two sides. Oake, you have every man left in this camp awake and on his toes. This night could decide many things."

Harley Dodd spurred away. Cass and his selected five began hurriedly saddling. Larkin brought in his own horse and did the same. Oake Calloway circled through the camp, giving out the word and men picked up guns and trooped out to form a tight guard circle.

The women of the camp gathered about the men for a final word. There was no wailing or complaining. They might know apprehension and fear for these men of theirs, but if they did they kept it deep inside them, and there was no attempt to hold any man from his duty.

Rose Calloway slipped up beside Cass Partee for a moment. Then, only when she stepped over to Britt Larkin, did this girl show what was in her heart. Her whisper was small, contained.

"Bring him back to me, Britt — !"

Larkin, wordless, dropped a hand on her arm and squeezed it.

They spurred away, cutting up from the valley floor to hit the sweep of clear grass land which lay between the first fringe of hill timber and the sage country below. Out along this they sped, with Larkin leading the way.

On one side in the far distance the lights of

Fort Cord were a faint glimmer. On the other the Royales lifted, black against the sky. Far out at the rim of the world a glow in the night sky told of the approach of a moon soon to rise.

Larkin kept to the driving pace for some distance, then angled up into the first edge of the timber. Here the pace slowed and men and horses were dark bulks, threading the forest aisles. Larkin was cutting for Three Link headquarters by the shortest, most direct line. But as time and distance slid away, he rode with increasing caution. He wasn't dead sure of anything. He could only close in carefully, testing the night with every straining sense, and gamble that fortune was smiling his way. Came a time when he reined in and dismounted.

"You men stay right here," he told Partee and the others. "I'm going to scout ahead on foot for a ways. No talking, no smoking. We don't know who is watching and listening and sniffing the air. We're playing this thing a little blind, and we don't want to jump too soon, or come up too late. Wait for me!"

He went off, angling up slope, the picture of this area cast sharply in his mind. Not too far from here ran the Three Link trail to town. He worked toward this and when he came up to it, crouched low against the bole of a big pine while he listened, keening the night.

The minutes ticked by and there was no sound or sign of movement. He was straightening up, prepared to step into the trail and move up it, when he heard the soft thump of hoofs from above. He dropped back, flattened down behind the bulk of the pine. The hoofs shuffled closer and then there were two riders, drifting down the trail. One of them was grumbling profanely.

"Lot of damn foolishness, this. You'd think Dutch was gettin' spooked, sendin' us down here to see if the valley was quiet. Of course it'll be quiet. Why shouldn't it be?"

"Dutch ain't gettin' spooked," defended the other. "He's just playin' it smart. No sense in takin' chances. He ain't forgettin' how Rufe and Mace and Neely were surprised and had their guns taken away from them a while back up in the parks. That showed these hills ain't empty of everybody but us. No sir, Dutch is playin' it smart."

They went on down the trail, the sound of their horses fading. Larkin got to his feet and moved higher up, not in the trail, but just off the edge of it. He traveled with slow care, a few steps at a time, then another stop to test the night once more. Of one thing now he could be certain. The attack was definitely to be on Three Link, but it wouldn't come until the two riders had reported back.

From here, Three Link headquarters lay only a scant half mile above. Anywhere along here now, Dutch Klymer would be waiting for the report of the two scouts he'd sent out. Larkin moved ahead, slipping from one black pillared tree trunk to another.

In the dark a horse sneezed, stamped restlessly. A man cursed at the animal and then there was the muted growl of voices. It was hard to pick out any particular voice, harder yet to catch any words clearly. Larkin flattened down and waited, the night pressing dark and close there in the timber.

In time, the shuffle of hoofs came back up the trail, and the two riders who had gone down the trail, now came back up it. As they passed the spot where Larkin lay, one of the horses snorted and shied. The rider of the animal hauled it to a stop and his voice hit out, curt and wary.

"What's that? Anybody there?"

Larkin held his breath. Then the second rider spoke scoffingly.

"For God's sake, Chet, what's the matter with you? Your bronc snorts over some damn wanderin' porkypine or somethin' and you get all your feathers on end. Never saw such a bunch of spooky hombres. Ever since we pulled out tonight it's been the same. Dutch is as bad as the rest of you. Anybody would think the night was set to sprout ten thousand horned devils."

The speaker rode on and his companion, with a muttered curse, followed him.

Ahead, a challenge was thrown at them and their answer carried clearly back to Larkin.

"Nothin' stirrin' in the valley, Dutch. Didn't think there would be."

Larkin also got the reply to this. It came with gravelly harshness.

"I'll do the thinkin'. Rest of you do as you're told. We'll move in now. Schell should be in position by this time."

Came the creak of saddle gear as men who had been afoot, stepped into their saddles again. Massed hoofs moved on up the slope, and the sound of them thinned and died. Larkin began drifting down slope again, angling away from the trail. He moved with caution for a little way, then stepped out faster as he put distance between himself and Klymer's crew. Soon he was taking long, plunging strides that were almost a run.

He came back to where Cass Partee and the others waited and his words were curt and hurried.

"They're there. And they're moving up now to attack. Come on!"

He went into his saddle with one smooth lunge, then led the way straight through to the Three Link town trail. Just as they broke into this, the thin, flat echo of a gun shot carried down from above. This was followed by a short pause and then the night was torn wide open with gun fire. The attack had begun. This thing was committed, now.

Larkin sent his horse up the trail at a hard, grunting run. Close behind, Cass Partee and the others hammered along. Just below the rim of the basin in which Three Link headquarters stood, Larkin cut off the trail to the right, circling under the rim a good hundred yards. There he pulled to a halt, swung from his saddle and jerked his rifle from the saddle boot.

"We go in on foot," he announced. "Klymer and his crowd rode in. So, anything you see in a saddle this side the headquarters buildings is fair game. Shoot it! For it's that kind of a night!"

They climbed the last few yards to the basin rim and on to the level beyond. Only a glance was needed to tell Larkin that Three Link had not been caught totally unprepared. All lights in the buildings were out, but there were rifles lashing from the dark bulks. Yet it was a pitifully thin line of defenders, for by this time Jesse Schell was hitting from above and Three Link was between two fires.

Larkin led the way at a crouching run, circling, aiming to come in at the lower side of the corrals, hoping to catch Klymer on the flank. Hoofs belted in front of him and a riderless horse raced by, empty stirrups swinging. Some one of the defenders had tallied.

Another horse came plunging, rearing and squealing, wild from the firing and the sting of a creased bullet wound. Its cursing rider was trying to fight it under control. Larkin tipped up his rifle and shot. The cursing broke off abruptly and there was the muffled impact of a body striking the ground. The crazed horse went racing on.

By now, Larkin had the over-all picture pretty well in mind. The yelling voices and the flashes of the guns gave it to him. Dutch Klymer's force had fanned out into a ragged line across the basin, milling a little, disconcerted by the unexpected resistance that had cropped up.

Cutting through the echoes of the guns, Larkin could hear Klymer's heavy shouts at his men, telling them to spread further and then close in. Kneeling, Larkin held low across that line of gun flashes and levered his rifle empty, its hard, spanging reports caught up and blended in more of the same as Cass Partee and the other squatters followed Larkin's example.

The effect was immediate. This raking, unexpected fire on their flank threw the attackers into confusion. A rider five yards away from Dutch Klymer, hurriedly reloading an empty gun, lurched as a bullet took him, toppled sideways out of his saddle. Almost at the same moment Klymer's horse, shot through the head, crumpled in its tracks and Klymer rolled free, barely in time to keep from having a leg trapped under his mount.

He came up raging. At first he thought he'd been caught in a cross fire by some of his own men. But immediately he knew that this couldn't be so. He saw the bunched flashes of the rifles over there to his right, close to the ground and he realized that this thing had gone wrong, that the surprise he and Jesse Schell had planned had been no surprise at all, and that they had ridden into something. He bawled at his men, cursing them.

"Get at that bunch yonder! Ride over 'em!"

There were some who tried, spurring straight in, with Klymer following them on foot, throwing shot after shot. But Larkin and his men were close to the ground and they had as targets men in saddles, bulking black against the stars. Two more horses went down. The charge broke up, scattered.

There came a queerly timed break in the tumult. And in that pause, echoing clearly down from the upper side of the basin came a high, thin, triumphant yell. Britt Larkin would have known that yell at any time and under any stress. He'd heard old Len Revis give it before, under the impulse of some great exultation. And it told him now that Len and the Dodd brothers and Sod Tremper had Jesse Schell on the hip.

A current of relief swept through Larkin. He'd figured this thing right, he hadn't made any mistakes. Now there was nothing else to do except carry this thing to a final, grim finish. He rose from his knee and headed in at a run toward the spot where Dutch Klymer's raging shouts were again lifting.

He heard a man groaning and cursing, off to one side, but paid no attention. For he knew that this snake had two heads, Klymer and Schell, and one of those heads was close to him. A rider fled by, heading for the safety of the basin rim. Larkin swung up his rifle but the gun clicked empty. Larkin dropped it, drew his belt gun.

He wasn't far from Klymer now. The renegade leader was raging at one of his men.

"Rufe! Damn you, Rufe — get me a horse!"

A rider spurred in. "Behind me, Dutch! Swing up behind me!"

They made a dark bulk, the horse and the two men, one in the saddle, the other trying to swing up behind. Larkin chopped two shots at them and the group broke apart, the horse rearing and pitching, rider still in the saddle, other man still afoot.

A gun lashed back at Larkin. Something that was like a white-hot edge of fire burned along his ribs and the shock of it spun him half off his feet. He recovered, staggering. The horse and its rider were plunging away. But in the first moon glow that now began to slant across the basin, Larkin saw the burly shadow that was Dutch Klymer, not ten yards distant.

"Klymer!" he challenged.

His answer was the blare of a gun and it was like an invisible hand tugging briefly at the open collar of his shirt, only inches from his throat. It seemed to Larkin that his own moves were suicidally slow. Yet his gun was up and level, the tip of it lost against that shadowy figure in front of him. He felt the weapon buck in recoil, then again.

The shadowy figure held its place for a throbbing moment. The steady cursing broke off in a coughing, moist gasp. Then the shadow went down, blending with the earth.

Off in the night a horse's running hoofs pounded and a voice was calling back.

"Dutch! Dutch — !"

But there was no answer save the final shot in Larkin's gun, which was wild and did no good. For the world had suddenly begun pitching up and down and to his numbed amazement Larkin found himself on the ground.

He half lay, half sat there, conscious now of the heavy, sticky moistness spreading under his shirt. He remembered now, that hot burn of lead along his ribs. Queer that he hadn't gone down then. But that was what fighting fury could do to a man. Prop him up and keep him going to some kind of a finish. . . .

Gunfire was sporadic, lessening. At the far edge of the basin there was still some of it going on, and it was being answered both from the dark ranch buildings and from behind and a little to Larkin's right, where Cass Partee and his group were bunched.

Again came a distant, questing yell. "Dutch! Give an answer, Dutch — !"

There was no answer. There never would be.

Then, abruptly as it had started, it was finished. Guns went silent. Two different voices were calling Britt Larkin's name. Tom Adin's, from up at the ranchhouse, and then Cass Partee's, over in back of him.

His mumbled answer reached Cass, and then there was Cass leaning over him, voice thin with anxiety.

"Britt! How bad, boy?"

"Scrape along the ribs. Give me a hand up. I

ought to be able to walk."

Cass helped him erect, then swore softly. "Maybe only a scratch, but you're minus some blood by the feel of this shirt."

Cass yelled over his shoulder. "Give a hand here, one of you. The rest bring Jim Dykes up to the ranchhouse."

"You mean," mumbled Larkin, "that Jim got it?"

"Just a leg. He'll be all right."

One of the squatters hurried up, and with a man on either side of him, Larkin stumbled across the basin toward the ranch buildings. Cass Partee sent a shout ahead.

"Hold your fire! Friends coming in."

Lights flickered and shone again from ranchhouse and bunkhouse. Tom Adin, rifle across his arm, came out to meet them. He heard Cass Partee's quick words of explanation, then led the way to the bunkhouse. They got Larkin on a bunk and Cass Partee began cutting away the blood soaked shirt. Alec Creager came in the door.

"Britt!" he exclaimed, alarm deepening his voice. "How bad is this?"

Larkin mumbled an answer. "I'll live to plague you some more, Alec."

Creager turned to his foreman. "We'll take care of Britt, Tom. You better make a scout. Klymer could come back for another try."

"You can forget Klymer, Alec," murmured Larkin, his eyes closed. "He'll never come back. He's dead. Out there in the meadow. Now, if

Len and the boys could have had the same luck with Jesse Schell — !"

A little later a generous slug of whiskey burned down Larkin's throat. Also, the hands that were working at his wounded side were softer and gentler than those of any man. He knew who it was, even before he opened his eyes and looked at her.

"Joyce," he said, "this is no work for you."

"Quiet!" she ordered gently. "I'm not as useless as you may think."

A twinge of pain made him flinch involuntarily. Her lips trembled. "I've got to hurt you a little, Britt. This wound must be cleaned. Now if you'll just lie still — !"

So he did, while some sort of cooling stuff was smeared on torn flesh, and then bandages packed and bound in place. After that it was good to just lie very still, not move or even think. A strange lassitude settled over him, seemed to press him deep into the blankets. The world slipped away from him.

When he awoke, there was sunshine slanting in at the bunkhouse door. He felt good, amazingly good. Good enough to get up. Until he tried it. Then he knew better and he settled back again with a grunt. Len Revis' voice came to him.

"That's right. Try and play it bull-headed and get yourself more misery. Stay put, or I tie you to that bunk."

Larkin turned his head and looked at Len, sitting in a nearby chair. They were alone in the bunkhouse. "Where's everybody?" asked Larkin.

"Here and yonder," informed Len. "Harley an' Chuck an' Sod Tremper are out lookin' for Jesse Schell an' Obe Widdens. They got clear away, damn 'em! Duke Nulk wasn't that lucky. Neither were two of Klymer's crowd who come in from above with Schell. Seein' as how you got Klymer, I'd say that combine was kinda busted up. This range went through the wringer last night and a lot of bad water was squeezed out."

Larkin considered soberly. "The luck couldn't have been all on our side."

"Wasn't," said Len succinctly. "There's you with those creased ribs, and that squatter, Jim Dykes, with a shot up leg. And Stony Cuff."

The way Len spoke this last name made Larkin swing his head again. "How bad with Stony?"

Len shrugged, turned up his hands. "After the ruckus quieted down and we counted noses, Stony wasn't there. We found him out by the corrals, where he'd been posted. He musta got it right when things first broke." Len touched his forehead. "He never knew what hit him." Len went on, his tone going gentle. "He was a good feller, Stony was. Never asked a damn thing of life except a chance to earn a honest livin' and the right to laugh when he felt like it."

For Larkin, the sunlight slanting in at the door

was not so bright as it had first seemed. He thought of the last time he'd seen Stony, when the cowboy had been riding line and had bummed a smoke off him. Stony was just as Len had described him. A plain, faithful, fun loving cow hand.

"Which side of the corrals, Len, upper or lower?"

"Upper. On our side. An' facin' that way when we found him."

"Jesse Schell's side?"

"Yeah. Jesse Schell's side. So, when we found Nulk and them two of Klymer's crowd, we never wept a drop."

"Jesse Schell," said Larkin softly, "has got a lot to answer for. I'm not done with that fellow." He lifted his head and looked around the bunkhouse again. "Jim Dykes. Where is he?"

"Cass Partee and those other squatter boys loaded him in Alec's spring wagon and took him down to the camp at the flats. Cass said they had an old feller down there who'd done some doctorin' in his early days and that he knew quite a bit about busted bones. An' Dykes was hurt that way."

Steps sounded at the door and Alec Creager came in, grave and tired. He looked down at Larkin. "How do you feel?"

"Fine, considering. A cup of coffee would go good."

Creager nodded. "Joyce will attend to that. Britt, I'm in debt to a lot of people. You, Len and the rest of your boys. The squatters, too. All of you. On its own, Three Link wouldn't have had a chance."

"It was everybody's fight, Alec. About Stony Cuff, I don't know what to say."

Creager's voice ran gruff. "There's nothin' anybody can say. All we can do is remember Stony as he was, a damn good man."

Larkin's lips pulled thin. "Too good to die because of a pair of rotten whelps like Jesse Schell and Dutch Klymer."

There was another step at the door, a soft one. Alec Creager threw a quick heartiness into his voice.

"Here's a man awake and yelling for food, Joyce. Can you do something about that?"

She stood for a moment in the doorway, looking at Larkin. There was a drawn paleness in her face and a deep, soft sadness in her eyes. Joyce had thought a lot of Stony Cuff, too. Now, without speaking, she nodded and slipped away.

Alec Creager took a turn up and down the bunkhouse. "That crowd was punished pretty wickedly, Britt. I doubt we'll have any more trouble from them. With Klymer done for, his gang is almost certain to break up and scatter. As for Schell — !"

Larkin lifted his arms restlessly, stretched, then winced at the stab of soreness in his wounded side. He said the same thing he'd said to Len. "I'm not done with that fellow."

"Nor I," said Creager harshly, "if I can locate

him. I sent Tom Adin and Race Wallace and Cotton Barr out to scout the Running S. I told them that if they got a chance to catch Schell over their sights to think of Stony Cuff and then use their own judgement."

The grizzled cattleman took another turn along the bunkhouse then stopped and stared out of a window. "Any man hates to end up a proven fool. But that's me. To think I ever considered Jesse Schell as a friend — !"

A little later Joyce came in again, carrying a small tray. There was plenty of hot coffee and a small dish of gruel. She pulled up a chair beside Larkin's bunk.

"You're having just what I think you ought to have," she said. "So don't howl for more. You won't get it."

Alec Creager and Len Revis slipped out. Joyce propped Larkin up on some pillows and he drank coffee and spooned gruel meekly. He tried to think of something to say which would drive that sadness from Joyce's eyes. She seemed to understand his thought, for abruptly her eyes brimmed and tears ran down her cheeks. Larkin captured one of her hands. He held it until the tears stopped. Her eyes told him she was grateful for his silence.

When he'd finished eating, Larkin grinned at her. "Be sitting up to a table for my next meal."

She tossed her head. "Indeed you won't. You'll do exactly as you're told, sir. Len Revis has his orders. From me."

"Tough," drawled Larkin. "Tough as whang leather. That's you."

She gathered up her tray and dishes, moved toward the door, meeting Larkin's word of thanks with just a hint of a wan smile. When she'd gone, Larkin built a smoke and settled back, knowing some content. In a small way he'd lightened her mood.

His cigarette smoked out, he dozed for a time, slept a little. When he woke again the warmth of midday lay in the bunkhouses. There were a couple of blue bottle flies buzzing drowsily up against the rafters and outside, in one of the pine trees, a crested jay was chattering.

There came the mutter of hoofs out by the corrals, then the sound of men's voices and the tinkle of approaching spur chains. Len Revis and Alec Creager and Tom Adin came in. Tom smiled down at Larkin.

"Got news for you, Britt. Running S has gone up in smoke."

"Running S! You mean burned?"

Tom Adin nodded. "That's right." He sat down on the neighboring bunk and got out his smoking.

"Them who were left of Dutch Klymer's crowd did it. Race Wallace and Cotton Barr and me, we saw the whole thing. We'd been scouting. We cut high and we cut low and finally we came up to Running S for a look. There were seven or eight riders there, packin' gear on their horses. They weren't wasting any time, either.

They pulled out in a bunch, heading high and back across the mountains where they came from.

"Race and Cotton and me, we watched them go. All of a sudden there was smoke showin' at the doors and windows of the ranchhouse. The bunkhouse was showin' smoke, too. There wasn't a thing Race and Cotton and I could do. All of a sudden the whole thing was one big bonfire. Wherever Jesse Schell is, he's got no headquarters to come back to."

"Even so, it was a wastrel thing to do," said Alec Creager harshly. "Damned renegade riff-raff — !"

"Their way of getting even with Schell," said Larkin slowly. "Jesse brought them in here on some kind of a deal. All they got out of it was to be well shot up, in addition to losing their leader, Dutch Klymer. So they hit back at Jesse that way before pulling out. Alec, let's not be foolish enough to weep over Jesse's hard luck."

A little later a buckboard came rolling up from the valley. Driving it was Rose Calloway. Tom Adin and Race Wallace and Cotton Barr were out by the corrals, catching up fresh horses to ride another patrol and see if they could find any trace of Jesse Schell. As Rose pulled her buckboard team to a stop, Tom Adin tipped his hat gravely.

"Britt Larkin?" asked Rose. "Is he truly all right?"

"Not exactly ready to climb into a saddle

again, ma'am," said Adin. "But he's comin' along first class."

"Do you think I could see him?"

Tom Adin smiled. "Can't think of a reason why you shouldn't." He pointed. "Yonder, in the bunkhouse."

Rose stepped from the rig and crossed toward the bunkhouse door.

Over in the ranchhouse kitchen, Joyce Creager was fixing another tray of food for Larkin. Sound of the buckboard rolling in caused Joyce to step over to an open window. Startled, she stood there motionless, watching Rose Calloway move up to the bunkhouse, pause at the door for a moment, then go in.

For some little time Joyce did not move. Then, when she finally did turned back to her chore, her manner was a little uncertain. But presently, spots of color blooming in her cheeks, her moves became brisk and sure again. And when, a little later, she left the house, carrying the tray, her head was high and there was the flash of almost combative purpose in her eyes.

Over in the bunkhouse, Britt Larkin had to blink to make sure he was seeing right.

"Rose!" he exclaimed. Then his look sharpened. "Don't tell me something has happened down in the valley? No trouble? No — ?"

Rose came quickly over beside him. "Nothing has happened, only worry over you. Cass said you'd been — been hurt, but not seriously. Yet, men can belittle such things and I wanted to be sure, to see for myself."

Her warm smile beamed down at him, but her eyes were faintly moist. It was, he thought, the goodness in her, the vast capacity of this girl to give of her sympathy and kindness.

"I'm all right," he said. "Just a little bullet burn across the ribs." Then he added, "It's mighty fine of you to come and see me."

She turned sober. "You kept your promise, Britt. You sent Cass back to me. For that — !"

She bent swiftly, brushed a kiss across his lips. Then, as she straightened up, she laughed softly. "My thanks, Britt. And that of all the women on the flats. For you sent all our men back to us. Jim Dykes, he's going to be all right, too."

There was a faint cough at the doorway. Then Joyce Creager came in, carrying her tray. Her smile was bright, a little too bright if studied carefully.

"Excuse me," she said. "But sick men must eat."

"I sure agree there," enthused Larkin. "Hope there's more than just that thin soup stuff like last time. You two recognize each other, of course. Joyce, this is Rose Calloway. Rose, meet Joyce Creager."

Rose said, "I'm very happy."

Joyce, not to be outdone, nodded. "And I. Shall we feed this man?"

Rose gave her soft laugh. "I'll leave that up to you, Miss Creager. I've got to be getting back to the flats. There is still a great deal of work down there for all of us. I just had to make sure that Britt was doing as well as I was told he was."

She moved to the door. "We'll be looking for you back with us, Britt."

Then she was gone and presently came the sound of receding buckboard wheels.

"That's Rose Calloway for you," said Larkin. "She drove all the way up here, just to say thanks. Imagine that."

"Yes," said Joyce crisply. "Just imagine." She punched some pillows into shape, punched them hard. "Sit up there and don't make a greedy pig of yourself just because there's more food than last time."

She lifted the tray from the bunkhouse table, put it on his lap and went out, her shoulders very straight.

Chapter XI

FRUITS OF TOIL

IT WAS a full week before Larkin was able to be up and around again for a little time each day. Even when Len finally helped him into his clothes, he found that his legs were weak and his head light. He swore sulkily over these things. Len grinned.

"And he was the bucko who thought he was going to bounce right back out of the blankets the morning after."

"Shut up!" snapped Larkin. "Bad enough to feel puny as an infant without you rawhiding me about it. Damned if I don't think you've enjoyed having me laid up."

"Have," admitted Len with smug complacency. "Riding herd on you in one place gave me a chance to catch up on my own rest."

Larkin looked around for something to throw at Len, and the old rider sauntered out, chuckling.

"Gettin' mean," Len told Joyce Creager a little later in the day. "Good sign. When they turn mean then they're beginnin' to feel their oats again. Give him a few days more and he'll be back in the saddle again."

Time dragged for Larkin and his side itched, which was also a good sign of healing. He ate heartily and he was constantly prodding Len for news.

"You're fuller of questions than a wooly dog is fleas," complained Len. "I told you forty times already that Harley and Chuck and Sod Tremper ain't been able to raise hide or hair of Schell an' Widdens. An' they been combin' the trails every day since you got laid up. They're still combin' 'em."

Other things contributed to Larkin's unrest. Joyce Creager, for one. Darned if he could understand the girl. She brought him his food faithfully, but now she just put it on the bunkhouse table and then went away again. When he tried to get her to stay and talk with him, she always came up with some excuse that she had work to do. And so she left him to stew in solitary bewilderment and disgust.

Evenings weren't so bad. Then Tom Adin and Race Wallace and Cotton Barr would be on hand, to talk and swap range gossip. They could bring him no more word of Jesse Schell than Len Revis had been able to. Apparently, Schell and Obe Widdens had cleared completely out of the country.

Came a day when Larkin was taking the sun outside the bunkhouse and Joyce Creager emerged from the ranchhouse with a basket of laundry, which she began hanging on a line. Larkin went over there.

"What's the matter with me?" he demanded bluntly. "I got the spotted fever?"

She looked at him over her shoulder. "I don't know what you mean."

"Oh, yes you do," he charged. "You stay away from me like I had the itch, or somethin'."

She turned back to the hanging up of laundry. "It's a busy world," she said. "Folks have things to do, including me. You can't expect to be babied forever."

Watching her, Larkin built a smoke. The damp laundry, warm and steaming in the sunlight, gave off a clean, sudsy smell. And Joyce, in gingham, was appealingly girlish.

"I'm not asking to be babied," Larkin grumbled. "But neither do I like to be treated like some stranger."

"Now," said Joyce, "you're being ridiculous." She picked up her empty basket and went back to the ranchhouse.

That night, Larkin made up his mind. He was up at crack of dawn the next morning, sneaking out of the bunkhouse and over to the corrals. He'd caught up his horse and was figuring how to toss up his saddle when Len Revis came up behind him, took the saddle out of his hand, swung it into place and began cinching it on.

"If you must travel," growled Len, "I guess now's as good a time to start as any. But no heftin' of a saddle for a few days yet. I'll do that for you. But don't you think you'd better stick around for breakfast an' thank a few folks?"

"Breakfast can wait and they all know how I feel without me saying it," said Larkin gruffly. "I got to start toughening up again."

"Fair enough," agreed Len. "Only don't try an' push things too fast. Else you'll end up needin' another spell of nursin'."

They rode off down slope. The breath of night still lingered in the timber, cool and moist and sweet, and Larkin luxuriated in it, drawing it deep into his lungs. He found that by shifting a little sideways in the saddle he could ride with reasonable comfort. Len moved up beside him.

"Reckon Jesse Schell's still in the country," said the grizzled puncher. "Harley and Chuck Dodd found the ashes of a campfire back up near the head of Aspen Crick. Sign showed there'd been two men there. Adds up to Schell and Widdens. Harley and Chuck picked up the trail and followed it some, but it petered out in the high cap rock."

"I figured that sooner or later we'd pick up some trace of Jesse," said Larkin. "We're not done with that hombre, Len. I told Alec Creager and Tom Adin that the other evening when they were in the bunkhouse talking it over with me. Alec sort of leaned to the idea that Jesse, now that his headquarters was burned, and knowing that everybody was on the lookout for him, had pulled stakes complete. I didn't agree. Jesse's got a one track mind, and he's just the sort to feel that getting even is more important than anything else. No, we haven't seen the last of Jesse Schell."

"There ain't too much he can do," said Len. "Without no headquarters, no outfit, no nothin'."

"He can still kill somebody," differed Larkin. "I'll never feel right about Jesse Schell until I see him on the end of a rope or in a hole six feet under."

"Can't rightly argue against that," admitted Len. "Then you want that me an' Chuck an' Harley an' Sod Tremper should keep on prowlin' the trails?"

"Just Sod," Larkin said. "Rest of us got another chore to do. By this time there should be some word in town for me from Turk Henderson regarding those white faces I wrote him about. And we'll have to be heading out for Button Willow to drive them in. So you go collect Harley and Chuck and bring them down to the squatter camp. Wait there for me."

When they broke from the timber into the open slope of the valley, the sun's first light was beginning to gleam. Len said, "See you later," and swung away, lining out for the home headquarters. Larkin went on down toward the river flats.

The warm odors of breakfast met him as he rode up to the squatter camp, stirring up a sharp hunger in him. Cass Partee spied him and let out a yell.

"Britt!"

They crowded around, voicing their gladness at seeing him again. It was a welcome that warmed Larkin all through. He squatted on his heels beside the Calloway fire and dug into the food which Rose brought him.

"Eat hearty, Britt," she told him. "You're still a little thin and peaked."

From Oake Calloway, Larkin got an up to the minute report on the big job. In another week, Calloway said, they'd be ready.

"Been a tougher chore than I figgered, gettin' that sluice gate just right. And that gate is almost as important as the dam. It's got to work and work right, or we'll have water runnin' loose all over the place. And too much water would be as bad as not enough."

After he'd eaten, Larkin sought out Jim Dykes. Jim lay on a pad of blankets, his leg splinted and bandaged. He was thin and gaunt, but his eyes were clear.

"How's it, Jim?" Larkin asked.

"Fine," was the answer. "Only a question of time. Then I'll be sound as ever."

Later, Larkin headed for town. He took it easy, surprised how his strength was coming back. A lot, he decided, depended on a man's mind. Laying around, for an active man, was even worse than the cause of the lay-up.

When he walked into Henry Castro's store, Castro said simply, "This makes it a good day, Britt, seeing you around again. Heard all about the attack on Three Link. Must have been quite a ruckus. But it sure cleared the air. What's Alec Creager think now?"

"Know's who his real friends are," said Larkin briefly. "He's with us all the way, Henry, ready to put up his share of the money if we want it. Any mail for me?"

There was some. The expected word from Turk Henderson was there and it told of work ahead.

"The start of my new herd of white faces is due in Button Willow on Thursday," said Larkin. "That means I got to shuffle along, Henry."

"Any word on Jesse Schell?" asked the storekeeper. "Wouldn't pay to figger Jesse all through, Britt."

"My own opinion," agreed Larkin. "I got one man watching the trails in the Royales. This trip to Button Willow and back will toughen me up so I can hit those high trails myself when I get back. I'm going to do that. I'm going to run Jesse into a corner if it takes six months to do it."

In a rocky pocket, not half a mile from the extreme crest of the Royales, Jesse Schell squatted on his heels and stared at a camp fire that had guttered down to a few fading coals. Across the fire from him, Obe Widdens worked the last few grains of tobacco from a limp, soiled muslin sack, then tossed the bag onto the coals where it began to char then burst into a brief period of flame. The cigarette Widdens tucked into his lips was thin and unsatisfactory. After a few fruitless puffs, Widdens cursed, threw it after the empty tobacco sack.

"We got to do somethin', Jesse. We're down to our last bite of grub an' plumb out of tobacco. We're doin' no good hangin' around up here. We stay here, we starve to death. We drop lower down an' we run a strong chance of stoppin' a slug any minute from anywhere. I say to hell with it! Let's cross the mountains an' forget the whole business."

"No!" The word was an eruptive growl in Jesse's thick throat. He slammed a heavy fist against his leg. "No, by God! I got range down there, and cattle. Nobody is goin' to run me away from what's rightfully mine. You hear me? Nobody! And," he added darkly, "I got debts to pay."

A big physical change had come over Jesse Schell. Constant movement, uncertain rest, lack of enough food, had taken some of the burly solidity out of him. Then there were the inner fires that had been eating at him since the disastrous night attack on Three Link. In that move he and Klymer had won nothing, lost everything. Klymer his life, Jesse his headquarters. And since then there had been nothing but dodging and hiding and running from retribution.

All of this had had its effect on Jesse. The muscles of his face had sagged into folds, loose and brutalizing. Deep lines bracketed his heavy lips.

His eyes were sunken from fatigue and bloodshot from the corrosion of frustrated hate and rage.

He spat thickly into the fire. "Tonight," he said hoarsely, "we ride into town. Tonight — late."

Obe Widdens stirred restlessly. "Wouldn't be smart. Let's not kid ourselves, Jesse. We're open game, now. We show ourselves in town, then the first man who sees us will draw a bead on us. I tell you, the only place we can draw a full breath and feel safe is a long way from Reservation Valley."

"Nobody's goin' to see us in town," Jesse growled. "I said we'd go in late, didn't I? Well, that's it. And when we get there we pull a couple of boards off the back of Castro's warehouse and help ourselves to a number of things. We'll get plenty of grub, and something else I've a mind about. After that, we'll take care of a couple of matters."

"Like what?" asked Widdens.

Jesse told him, and with the telling a gleam came into Obe Widdens' eyes. There was little imagination in Widdens, but he could see a picture when some one else outlined it for him. And he'd ridden so long for Jesse Schell he'd got in the habit of letting Jesse do most of his thinking for him. The things Jesse now proposed appealed to the sly, prowling streak of ruthlessness which lay in Widdens. He nodded.

"Right with you, Jesse."

They sought sunlight and fitfully dozed the hours of daylight through. With the coming of twilight they caught up their horses, saddled and headed down toward the valley. They took it easy, letting the horses set their own pace at a walk. They rode wide, coming into the valley far to the west, then circling across the dark miles to come in on Fort Cord from the south. The hours of the night ran away, and when they finally reached the edge of town, Fort Cord was dark and silent. Even the lights of the Guidon were out.

Henry Castro's warehouse was part of the old military structure, stoutly enough built at one time, but now weakened under the ravages of time and weather. So Jesse and Widdens had no great difficulty in prying loose a couple of boards, making an opening big enough for a man to slip through.

They worked slowly and with care, making little noise beyond the complaining creak of a rusty nail or two being pulled from long occupied sockets. Inside the place the air was warm and redolent with the mingled odors of various kinds of merchandise. Using a match for a light, Jesse located an open and partially filled box of tallow candles. He lighted one of these, handed it to Widdens, then lit one for himself. By the glow of these they went to work.

They found a couple of empty gunny sacks and used these for containers. One of the sacks they stuffed with food supplies, the other Jesse used for other items. Shortly they were ready to go. Nearby was a stack of cased five-gallon cans of kerosene. Obe Widdens touched one of these with his toe.

"We could sprinkle some of that stuff around, drop a match and give this damned town something to think about, Jesse."

Schell cursed him softly. "Don't be such a damn fool! What good would that do? Our time to make the big fuss will come later, where it will count. Watch yourself with that candle! Don't let it drip. We don't want Castro to know anybody's been prowlin' in here. Not for a while, anyhow. After that, it won't matter a damn."

They went out the way they had entered and Schell carefully fitted the boards back into place and with a rock wadded up in a filthy handkerchief, softly tapped the nails back in place. When they rode away, the town still slept.

White faced cattle, glad to be free of the confines of the cars that had brought them to Button Willow, faced the north and plodded out the slow miles. Not a very big herd this, but all pure bred stuff. Given time, in numbers it would grow.

Back in the drag, Britt Larkin ate dust and didn't mind. Physically he was his old self again. His wounded side had healed and, aside from a slight tenderness, gave him no trouble. In this land a man either died or recovered quickly. And Larkin was vitally alive once more, lean and brown and knowing quickening enthusiasm every time he looked at the stocky, solid cattle moving out ahead of him.

The miles were long and slow, but they dropped behind, one by one. Each night, when Larkin rolled into his blankets, he was impatient for the night to pass, so he could get again at the drive. For he was eager to see these cattle in the high parks of the Royales. Once they were there, it meant another part of the great dream nailed down to fact.

The day came when the white faces plodded into Reservation Valley, the first of their breed ever to put hoof on this land. They filed by, just beyond the edge of Fort Cord. Larkin let Len Revis and the Dodd brothers keep the herd moving, while he cut into town.

Alec and Joyce Creager stood on the porch of Henry Castro's store. Larkin, gray with dust, beat the worst of it from his clothes and greeted them, smiling.

"White faces, Alec," he said. "The pure quill. Go take a look at those beauties and you'll forever after be ashamed of that cross breed mongrel stuff you been calling beef cattle."

Creager cleared his throat harshly, but his eyes twinkled. "Don't get too proud, Britt. I ain't rightly made up my mind yet, whether my new herd will be Herefords or Durhams. There's some who claim the Durham the best. They could be right." He looked Larkin over. "You weren't this spry and bouncy last time I saw you."

"A saddle man belongs in a saddle, not lying useless on a bunk," said Larkin. "Which reminds me that I owe plenty of thanks to you folks for letting me clutter up the premises like I did at Three Link. Consider them given."

Creager snorted. "Man, don't talk foolish."

Larkin turned to Joyce. She was standing reserved and quiet. "If you don't want the thanks, Alec, then I give them all to the one who nursed and fed me." He hesitated, then added, "I shouldn't have run out on you the way I did, Joyce. But at the time it seemed like a good idea."

She shrugged. "Perhaps it was. All I did was my duty."

A wagon rolled away from Henry Castro's warehouse, driven by one of the squatters. Henry Castro, frowning a little, locked the warehouse door and came along to the store.

"I must be gettin' old, or forgettin' how to count," he remarked. "I'd have sworn there were eight boxes of blasting powder left in the warehouse — full ones. But when I went out to get a couple for that squatter, there were only seven full ones. The other was half empty. I don't remember breaking it open."

"Man's entitled to count wrong or forget, once in a while, Henry," said Larkin. "Oake Calloway sent in for the powder?"

Castro nodded. "Understand the sluice gate is finished and he's ready to blow the lateral any time. But they want you present."

"In that case I don't see a thing wrong with tomorrow. I know how anxious those folks are to see water on the land they've cleared. I'm anxious myself, for that matter." Larkin turned to Creager. "Alec, I'd like to see Three Link present at the big moment. How about it?"

Creager considered, then nodded. "Three Link will be there, Britt. Don't deserve it, maybe. But we'll be there." Then, to Castro, the ranchman said, "Got a few things I want to pick up, Henry."

He and Castro went into the store, leaving Larkin and Joyce alone. The girl was looking out at the funneled up dust above the plodding herd of white faces.

"You certainly believe in building your own world, don't you, Britt?" she said.

"Put it that it's just my place in the world I want to build," he corrected. "The way you say it makes me a selfish whelp."

She flashed a quick glance at him. "I didn't mean it that way, and you know it. Why do you persist in misunderstanding me?"

Larkin spun up a smoke. "I'd like nothing better than to be able to understand you. I've been trying to for a long time, now. And just about when I think I'm getting close to the answer, I find I'm not. Maybe it's because I'm stupid."

She faced him, color flashing across her cheeks. "Maybe you are," she said crisply. Then she stepped past him and went into the store.

Larkin stood for a little time, dragging deep on his cigarette. Then he spun the butt into the street's warm dust, went to his horse and rode away after the white face herd.

He stayed with the cattle until they had watered at the river. Then, when the herd plodded on toward the nearing slope of the mountains, he cut away and headed for the squatter camp up river.

The first people he saw were Cass Partee and Rose Calloway. They were busy with some wooden stakes and lengths of string, driving the stakes into the ground, sighting along them and stretching string between them. Cass and Rose greeted him with their usual cheer.

"Time you're showing up," said Cass. "Everybody's anxious to see water in the ditch, but Oake won't blow the lateral until you're on hand."

"Tomorrow's the day," said Larkin. He twisted, slouching sideways in his saddle. "Just what do you two think you're doing? Laying out something for the kids to play hop-scotch in?"

Cass looked at Rose, smiled. "Hardly. We're layin' out our house."

"House!"

"That's right," nodded Cass. "Right here we build it. The day water comes down to these flats, Rose and me are gettin' married. What do you think of that?"

Larkin looked at them, from one to the other. Cass was all one big grin. Rose was smiling, too.

A little breathless, color warming her cheeks.

"Then it will be tomorrow," said Larkin softly. "Lucky, lucky people!"

Chapter XII

DEEP HILLS

NIGHT OVER the valley, over the mountains, over the river gorge. A night without a moon, and the stars so high and far their light seemed dimmed. On a little flat far up along the rim of the gorge, Jesse Schell and Obe Widdens cooked and ate a frugal evening meal and then, by the fitful light of their small, sheltering fire, made their preparations.

Three bundles of pale brown, paper wrapped, oily looking cylinders of about the size and shape of tallow candles, tied firmly together. From each bundle a length of black fuse extended. Jesse Schell surveyed the dynamite charges with heavy satisfaction.

"We set these in the right places and we'll lift that dam out by the roots. Which ought to discourage a flock of squatters and blow Mister Larkin's fine scheme to hell an' gone."

"They can always build another one," pointed out Widdens.

"Maybe. Question of money enters there.

Question of a lot of things enters there. Can you name a better way of hittin' back?"

Obe Widdens didn't argue the point. He knew it would be useless. When Jesse got settled on an angle, there was no talking him out of it. Yet Obe was queerly uneasy. There was a strong streak of superstition in this lank, bony headed rider. He was a devout believer in the workings of luck. When a man's luck was right, then he could do anything and get away with it. But when it was wrong — !

Obe wasn't sure about their luck just now. It had been running increasingly bad since that day when he and Duke Nulk and Clint Crowder had hung the body of that squatter, Jed Sharpe, to the ridge pole of Britt Larkin's cabin. Now Duke Nulk and Clint Crowder were dead. And he was on the dodge, like some damned wolf with a bounty on its head.

When Jesse Schell had first outlined this scheme about blowing the dam, it had sounded fine. Maybe that was because it offered something to do besides skulking from one high pocket in the cap rock to another, out of food, out of tobacco, full of physical miseries and discomforts. Yeah, Jesse's idea had sounded pretty good, then. But now Obe wasn't so sure. Because he wasn't sure about his luck.

"Mebbe they'll have guards out, Jesse," he suggested.

Jesse grunted scoffingly. "Why should they? Not any more. Klymer's done for. You and me, by the trails we've left, are supposed to be hidin' somewhere up in the high peaks. Why should they figger they got anything to guard against, now? Don't act so damned spooky. I know what I'm doin'."

They hung their sack of food to the limb of a tree, saddled up, stamped out the fire and rode down along the rim of the gorge. They rode slowly, for the night was still young and they had all the dark hours ahead of them.

In a small stand of timber back from the rim, some quarter mile above the dam, they pulled up, dismounted and tied horses. From there they went on foot, over to the rim, where a steep side gulch made descent to the bottom of the gorge possible.

From below the soft wash of water carried up to them, and the breath of it lifted, moist and chill. In some far distance a coyote mourned and nearer at hand a screech owl clacked its bill and gave out its fretful, whimpering cry.

Sounds in and of the night. Signs, too, as Obe Widdens interpreted them. Not good signs. That damned owl, whimpering and complaining like some disembodied spirit. . . .

Obe licked dry lips. "Should they happen to have guards out — !"

Jesse turned on him, cursed him roughly. "What the hell's the matter with you? Lost your guts completely? I thought you figgered yourself a real salty hombre? Get out of the way! I'll go down first. And if there are any guards, you got a gun, ain't you?"

They went over the rim and down the side gulch, moving slowly and feeling their way.

At the squatter camp, old Sod Tremper hadn't been able to get to sleep. Late that afternoon he'd come down out of the mountains with a pack horse load of fresh beef, destined for the barbecue and celebration of the morrow and had decided to spend the night at the valley camp.

The rest of the camp, weary from the long weeks of driving toil, was asleep. No guards were out, for after the affair at Three Link, which had left Dutch Klymer dead and his gang scattered, and with Jesse Schell a fugitive in the mountains, there existed no further need of a guard.

During the series of night watches which Sod and Len Revis had spent above the Running S, the old squatter had come to like the night. The vast silence of it brought a man a feeling of peace and gave him a chance to think.

Sod got out of his blankets, pulled on his boots. Sheer habit made him pick up his rifle. He made a complete circle of the camp, his keen old senses instinctively sharp and alert. But the night was empty, the night was still, and there was no threat anywhere. But Sod wasn't ready to go back to his blankets just yet, so he turned off up slope and climbed toward the mouth of the gorge.

Near the falls he stopped for a time, listening to the steady splash of the lessened waters. A good sound, that. Wasn't nothing on earth that could take the place of water. Where water ran there was life. That's what water did to the earth, it fed it and made things grow.

As long as he'd come this far, Sod decided, he'd go on up to the dam. Wouldn't be much to see in the dark, but it would be kind of good to sit by that dam all by himself and think of what it was going to mean to a lot of people. His people.

He went in quietly and settled down on a handy rock fragment. He got out his old pipe, filled it with rough cut and tamped it down with a gnarled forefinger. He was reaching for a match when a single small foreign sound reached him. The click of one disturbed rock striking another. It came from up gorge, along the edge of the pond.

Sod pocketed his pipe, slid his rifle up across his arm, thumbing the hammer back. Then he waited. Again he heard sound, that of stumbling movement and a muffled cursing.

Sod stood straight up, rifle lifting to his shoulder. The movement up above became more than sound. With the keen, strained focusing of all his senses, Sod saw, in the faint star glow which filtered into the gorge, a dark bulk which broke and became two parts. Men!

Sod swung his rifle into line and his voice rang harsh. "Who is it? Speak up! I got a gun on you!"

For a small second there was complete, suspended silence. Then a strangled curse of surprise and those dark bulks that were men melted down into earth's blackness. Came a pencil of stabbing gun flame and heavy, thudding report. Another gun blared and echoes belted back and forth across the gorge.

Sod Tremper shot back, levering his rifle again and again, trying for those gun flashes, the reports of his rifle higher, sharper, more ringing than the others. A bullet, skidding off a rock, ricocheted up over the gorge rim in a banshee wailing. Another, smashing into rock close beside Sod, spattered him with stinging lead splinters. And then another hit him fairly in the center of his gaunt chest.

The blow was savage and drove the old squatter back a full stride. A draining numbness swept all through him. He tried to stay up there, tried to swing the lever of his rifle again. But sight was leaving him, sound was leaving him. He coughed softly, once. Then the rifle fell from his hands and he followed it down, crumpled and still.

Again came silence, heavy, oppressive. Then Jesse Schell's voice, tight and snarling.

"Just the one, and he's done for. Come on — get that dynamite set!"

"Hell with it!" droned Obe Widdens. "Let's get outa here. I knew our luck was still bad. Knew it — !"

He would have started back the way they came, but Jesse grabbed him, whirled him around. Jesse's words rang wildly savage. "No you don't! You try and run out on me now, you get the next slug."

"The sound of that shootin' will carry," argued Widdens desperately. "We'll have that whole damn squatter camp on our necks before we know it. I tell you, Jesse, our luck's bad!"

"We got time. Let's get at it!"

Jesse caught up the sack he'd been carrying, shoved Obe along with his other hand. They fell into the lateral cut, came out the other side, drenched and cursing, Jesse barely managing to keep the sack out of the water. They stumbled and floundered their way under the face of the dam. Here was more water, seeping, sliming rocks to slipperiness.

Down on the flats shouts were lifting. Obe Widdens had been right in one thing; the sound of the guns had carried.

"I told you," panted Obe. "I told you! They'll be on our necks — !"

Jesse paid him no attention. By feel alone he placed the dynamite charges, trying to get them in toward the base of the dam between the chunks of rock. One he dropped and couldn't find it again in the dark. Another he shoved into a hole among the rocks that was deeper than he thought and it fell beyond his reach. But he managed to find a place for the third. Then he reached for a match and began to curse. That fall into the lateral cut had soaked every one he had in his pockets.

But he remembered his hat, he always carried a few, tucked into the band of his hat. He had to try three of these before he could bring one sputtering to light. He held the uncertain flame to the end of the fuse until it began to hiss and give off small sparks and a thin line of acrid smoke. Then he lunged away.

They got back across the lateral. Obe Widdens was a fleeing, stumbling shape in front of Jesse. They reached the mouth of the side gulch and were clawing their way toward the top when the explosion came. Bursting light, bursting thunder. Echoes that rolled and bellowed and whooped. Then the dark again, and the breathless, shaking night.

"Did it, by God!" exulted Jesse. "Did it! Now one more chore, then we'll go across the mountains. But we'll come back, with enough men ridin' with us to take care of everything!"

It had been an evening of deep content for Britt Larkin. Along with Len Revis and Chuck and Harley Dodd, he'd pushed the new herd of white faces up along the timber slopes and into the high park where Tin Cup headquarters stood. Now the cattle were grazing all across the open expanse and Larkin stood before his cabin, watching them in the soft light which followed sundown.

Len Revis, his sleeves rolled up and an old flour sack tied about his waist as an apron, stole a moment from his supper cooking chore to come out for a look himself.

"Pretty, eh boy?" he observed. "Makes me think back to when you first started talkin' about white faces on our range. You had the picture clearer than I did, but I can sure see now what you meant. Considerable water's run under the bridge since that day."

The Dodd brothers, who had been putting up the horses, came over and had their look, and liked it. "One of them is worth four of the kind we used to chouse," said Harley. "And that goes for here or at trailhead in Button Willow."

They went in and ate supper, then sat around and talked about the new herd and built big plans for the future handling of it. It was Larkin who finally stretched and yawned.

"Better turn in, boys. Big day tomorrow down in the flats. And we got to be there to help celebrate."

Sleep came easy, what with the carryover of fatigue from the drive in from Button Willow.

It was a distant, deep thud of sound which broke through Larkin's consciousness and brought him awake. He pushed up on one elbow, listening, and caught the remaining rolling tempo of far-off echoes. It brought Len Revis and Harley Dodd awake also, though Chuck continued to snore.

"What in hell — ?" blurted Len. "What was that?"

"Something blew up," said Harley Dodd. "Sounded like one of those blasts Oake Calloway's been setting off in the gorge."

"Calloway wouldn't be settin' off any blasts in the middle of the night," growled Len.

Larkin shoved aside his blankets, swung his feet to the floor. "No, Oake wouldn't. But somebody else might have." He began yanking on his boots. "Something's wrong. Let's get down there!"

Harley shook Chuck awake and they scrambled into their clothes. Outside night was thick and dark and they had a little time of it before they got horses caught up and saddles in place.

Larkin was remembering now, something Henry Castro had said yesterday afternoon in town. Something about a box of blasting powder in his warehouse, broken open and half of the contents gone. At the time Larkin had paid small heed, making some joking remark. But now — !

They struck the valley trail and went down it at a run. When they hit the open slope, Larkin headed directly for the mouth of the gorge. Down there faint pin points of light were twinkling, moving. Squatters, carrying lanterns, hurrying into the gorge.

You couldn't ride a horse in there. So Larkin and his crew left theirs and scrambled along the narrow trail. The last of the flickering lanterns had vanished into the gorge. But now, as Larkin came past the point, he saw the lanterns and the shadowy figures of men grouped. Voices rang, hard and angry. Larkin pushed into the group.

A man, kneeling by something and swinging a lantern back and forth, got to his feet.

"It's Sod Tremper," he announced harshly. "An' he's dead, shot through and through. Last I saw of him last evening, he was turnin' in for the night. He musta got restless and decided to take a little prowl up here. And he run into — this — !"

Down below the face of the dam two other lanterns were flickering, moving back and forth. A man at the edge of the group around Sod Tremper called.

"How's it look, Oake?"

"Not too bad," came the harsh answer. "Some water is gettin' through and we'll have to do some fixin'. Whoever made the try at blowin' this dam didn't know too much about how powder acts. Force blew away from the dam instead of under it."

Oake Calloway and Cass Partee came up from their examination of the damage. In the lantern light, Calloway saw Larkin, and shook his head grimly.

"My fault, Britt. Figgered with Dutch Klymer done for and Jesse Schell on the dodge, we had nothin' left to fear. But somebody made a try at our dam. Who, I wonder?"

"Who else but Jesse?" said Larkin. He told Calloway about Henry Castro's remark concerning missing powder. "It adds up," he finished. "A night raid on Castro's warehouse. Easy to break into that old building. It's the way Jesse would reason, Oake. Anything to try and get even. And this ain't your fault any more than it's mine. We both been thinking too much of getting other things done, instead of going all out to take care of Schell. We don't make that mistake again. Len, Harley, Chuck — we ride!"

They left the gorge and went back to their horses. Night was not so black, now. In the east the sky was beginning to pale and stars were fading. Dawn was close at hand.

"Which way?" asked Len Revis.

"The gorge rim," said Larkin. "Jesse must have come down from above. We hit his trail now it'll be plenty fresh. And this time we don't let go of it until we come up with him, if we have to ride across three states to do it!"

They went up the slope and into the timber and angled from there toward the rim of the gorge. Gray daylight was breaking all about them. Ruddy color banded the eastern sky. A blue grouse, startled from its night roost, exploded into flight not a yard above and ahead of Larkin. His horse shied wildly, tangled with a down log and went to its knees. When it lunged up again, the animal was limping, favoring the near front leg.

Larkin swore softly, quieted the animal, got off and examined the leg.

"Acts like a strained tendon," he said as he straightened up. "Which means the bronc can't stand up to a long, hard trail. I'll have to cut back to headquarters and switch my saddle. Tell you what. When I get a fresh bronc, I'll ride high, for the cap rock. I'll pick a spot from where I can watch a lot of country. Maybe we'll get Schell between us. If nothing shows in a reasonable space of time, I'll drop down, pick up your trail and catch up with you later. You locate Jesse's trail, stay with it!"

"That," nodded Len Revis, "you can bet on. If we don't show higher up, then you better pick up a sack of grub, Britt, before you start to follow us. This thing could work into a long jaunt."

"I'll bring it," said Larkin.

The others moved on into the timber and Larkin cut back toward headquarters. His horse showed an increasing limp as he went along, so Larkin dismounted and led the animal. Larkin was restless with a grim impatience, his thoughts running somber.

It had been a mistake to let up at all on the initial chase of Jesse Schell. He should, he thought, have let everything else go until Jesse had been run to earth. Because he hadn't, another good man, old Sod Tremper, was dead, and only a break of undeserved luck, plus Jesse Schell's ignorance in how powder would act, had kept the dam from being completely destroyed. Well, it wouldn't be a mistake that would be repeated. . . .

In the quickening light of this new day, Jesse Schell and Obe Widdens worked a cautious way in toward Britt Larkin's Tin Cup headquarters. Here Jesse determined on a final strike of vengeance before heading out across the Royales. It was a plan he'd been figuring on all through the night past. First he'd blow the dam, then he'd take care of Larkin's headquarters. Burn Running S, would they? Well, two could play at that game.

Jesse didn't know the truth about the burning of his Running S. It never entered his head that the job had been done by the remnants of Dutch Klymer's crowd. For Jesse had been on the dodge that day, miles from the Running S. He'd seen the smoke and later got close enough to see his headquarters just a black ruin. And his natural assumption had been that Larkin and the squatters and Alec Creager were responsible.

So now he'd give Larkin the same dose, given a break of luck. And at some later day, when he'd rounded up another tough crew, he'd come back across the Royales and take care of Creager. He'd take care of everything.

That was the groove Jesse's thoughts were running in; a groove obsessed with the purpose of revenge, of getting even. He rode ahead, with Obe Widdens following.

Now that he was back in the saddle again, Obe Widdens had steadied somewhat. Things hadn't gone too bad, back at the dam. There had been a guard out, but he and Jesse had taken care of that, and Jesse had managed to set off the blast. Neither he nor Jesse had hung around long enough to find out the results of the blast, but Widdens, knowing no more than Jesse did about the action of powder, carried the same conviction Jesse did, which was that the dam had been successfully blown. So Widdens was satisfied on that score.

He wasn't too strong for this try at Tin Cup headquarters. He'd have been quite satisfied with the night's work just as was. But he knew it was useless to try and sway Jesse from his final purpose, and as long as it was there was nothing else to do but trail along warily, impatient to see it done, so they could get at the long ride to safety across the mountains. He had asked Jesse one question. What if they didn't find Tin Cup deserted?

"It will be," said Jesse with positive heaviness. "Blew the dam, didn't we? What'll the squatters do? Come runnin' and cryin' to Larkin, of course. Which means Larkin and his crew will be down there in the flat, addin' their tears to the rest. We hit 'em and we hit 'em good this trip, Obe. Right where it hurts."

They came in on the clearing cautiously and had their careful look from the shelter of the timber. Jesse exclaimed triumphantly.

"What did I tell you? Not a single damn saddle on the pole. The place is empty. Larkin and his crowd are down on the flats. Come on!"

Sun's first golden light was slanting across the tree crests when Britt Larkin reached the edge of the home clearing. There he stopped abruptly, spun back into the timber, pulling his limping mount with him. He swung around, dragged his rifle from its saddle boot, then left his horse and stole back to the timber edge for another look.

Over there, in front of his cabin, two saddle mounts stood. And even as Larkin paused for his first watchful moment, a lank figure stepped from the cabin door. Obe Widdens!

Obe had a well stuffed flour sack in his hands and now, after a quick look around the clearing, tied the sack behind the cantle of his saddle, took another look around, then went back into the cabin. Putting together this sack of grub had been Obe's idea. The ride across the Royales was a long one.

Just inside the edge of the timber, Britt Larkin was running, making a partial circle, getting closer to the cabin and coming up on its blind side. When he gained this spot he broke into the open and drove straight for the cabin. He went fast, for he could see a thin haze begin to seep from under the eaves. Smoke!

It was sight of that smoke which awakened the cold fury in him. Until now the feeling had been one of merely grim purpose, and he had figured his moves for the day logically. Jesse Schell had proven himself a menace that had to be destroyed for the good of the valley. And Larkin had set himself to the chore much as he would have if it called for the running down of a timber wolf cattle killer. But sight of that smoke set him off.

The intrinsic value of the cabin wasn't great. But it had been home to him for a long time. It had sheltered him in storm. It had been a place of comfort to come to after a long and weary day of work. And no matter how humble a dwelling might be, a man could not know its shelter and build his dreams within its walls, without it becoming almost a part of him. That was the way Britt Larkin felt about this cabin of his, and now Jesse Schell and Obe Widdens were looting and burning it.

For Larkin knew that Jesse was in there. He had to be. Where Obe Widdens was, there would Jesse be. And no doubt it was Jesse who had touched off the fire. . . .

Larkin came up to that blind side of the cabin, panting thickly. The bloom of smoke around the eaves had thickened. There was enough of it so that it ran in little rippling sheets before the slow drift of the morning breeze. Larkin stepped past the cabin corner, so he could see the door. Obe Widdens came out the door, followed by a blooming blob of smoke. Obe had his head turned, was yelling at Jesse.

"Come on, man — come on! You got it started good enough. This thing'll be a torch in five minutes. And we got to get out of here!"

Larkin, half crouched, sent his own words at Widdens.

"You've waited too long, Obe. Too long — !"

Widdens came around, mouth half open, eyes quick and startled. He saw Larkin, saw the rifle Larkin held. Saw the relentless purpose in Larkin.

Obe Widdens tried to do three things at once. He was successful in only one of them. He yelled, "Jesse — look out! Larkin — !"

Then he dragged at his gun and tried to lunge back into the cabin.

The snarl of Larkin's rifle was a sharp and vibrant echo across the clearing. There was a force that spun Obe Widdens half around, drove him against the door post of the cabin. He seemed to hang there for a moment, then he doubled at the waist and piled up in a shrunken heap on the cabin's low step.

Larkin dropped his rifle, drew his belt gun and waited, watching the empty doorway. His own yell lifted harshly.

"That's it for Widdens, Jesse! You're next, Jesse. Come on out. I'm waitin' for you!"

Jesse Schell had been savoring to the full his destruction of Larkin's cabin. It offered a vent for his hate. He'd yanked bed ticks from the bunks, ripped them open, heaped the dried grass contents in the center of the floor and set them afire. Then he'd torn and smashed up everything he could and piled it on the blaze. Grub shelves above the stove, center table and benches, all he had broken and tipped and shoved until they were on the pile and the flames beginning to lick up around them.

Even when the smoke thickened to the place where it was beginning to gag in his throat and make him cough, Jesse went on with his orgy of destruction. Every time he ripped something apart, it was as though it was Larkin personally he was working on.

Then came Obe Widdens' wild yell of warning. And then a gun's snarling report. And now, where was Obe — where was Obe — ?

Jesse had started for the door, a big, feral shape, plunging through the smoke, when Larkin's yell reached him. And that yell brought Jesse up short, jarring him back to his senses. It was as if a deluge of icy water had hit him. Larkin — Britt Larkin, was outside that door, waiting with a ready gun! Larkin and how many others?

Panic gripped Jesse Schell. That door — what waited for him outside that door? Maybe there was some other way out. That rear window, beyond the stove. But the fire was between him and the window now. It had spread across bone dry boards of the floor, was already licking up log walls, equally tinder dry. It was spreading with terrifying rapidity, this consuming red monster he'd brought to life with one small match. A pitch pocket in a log exploded with a small, spiteful report and the flames licked greedily at the exposed resin.

Echoing in past the rising voice of the flames came another yell from Britt Larkin.

"Waiting for you, Jesse! Or you can stay in there and roast. You started it!"

Jesse whirled, tried to kick the flaming pile on the floor apart. All he did was spread and loosen it and the flames shot higher.

Heat scorched him, smoke choked him. The fire was a red demon, mocking him, reaching hungry, consuming tongues at him. With a strange and blubbering cry, Jesse whirled and charged out the door. There was too much pain in fire. . . .

Jesse had his gun in his fist and he was shooting blindly, crazily. An answering bullet took him from the side, sending him lurching. He kept his feet, turned that way, shooting — shooting. He saw Larkin, just as Larkin's gun leaped in recoil a second time.

The slug lifted him on his toes, seemed to hold him there. The gun in his own hand clicked on an empty cylinder. Then a third slug took him — and a fourth — !

He was a burly, dying thing. Going down. Down to his knees, down on his face. Down to nothing. . . .

Britt Larkin did things mechanically. He dragged Obe Widdens from the doorstep of the cabin. Then he backed away and watched his cabin die, too. There was nothing he could do about that. Little tongues of crimson were beginning to sprout on the split shakes of the roof.

For some reason, Britt Larkin was suddenly deathly weary. He sat on the ground, folded his arms on his bunched up knees, dropped his head on his arms. Once, so very long ago, it seemed, he'd found much in life to laugh about. He wondered if he ever would again — ?

Chapter XIII

THE HEALING TOUCH

LEN REVIS and the Dodd brothers had had little trouble in picking up the trail of Jesse Schell and Obe Widdens. They struck it at the head of the side gulch where Schell and Widdens had gone down into and come out of the gorge proper. They found where Schell and Widdens had left their horses. And as they worked out the trail, they found it leading them back around the mountain slope in the general direction of Tin Cup headquarters.

Len Revis pondered this with growing uneasiness. "Don't know what the devil Jesse and Widdens would be wantin' to head this way for," he growled. "But Britt's headin' for home to pick up that fresh bronc and should he bump into them two with the odds against him — ! I'm for cuttin' straight for home. If everything is all right there, we can come back here and pick up the trail again."

"Right!" said Harley Dodd.

They spurred away on a direct line, cutting

short slants through the timber, dodging the heavier thickets of jackpines. And abruptly Len Revis lifted high in his saddle, for faintly coming in out of the distance ahead, was the muffled echoes of gunfire.

"Knew it!" Len cried. "Had a feelin'. God damn it — ride!"

Now they really used the spurs, and when they finally hit the benchland that led to the open park, their mounts were foaming and laboring. They smelled the smoke before they saw the flame, and a gray, drained look came over Len's seamed, leathery face.

When they broke into the open park the cabin was a solid pyre of flame. They saw this and they saw Britt Larkin crouched down some fifty yards from the fire. And then, when Larkin got to his feet and faced them, something perilously close to a sob of relief broke from old Len Revis' lips.

Len left his saddle while his horse was still running. "Britt! You're all right?"

"The cabin, Len," said Larkin woodenly. "They burned our cabin."

"Hell with the cabin!" exploded Len. "We can always build another. But you — ?"

"Never touched me," said Larkin, in that same emotionless tone. "Widdens never had a chance, and Jesse was shootin' wild and crazy."

Now Len saw the two bundles of clothes that had once been men. He walked over to each, looked, then came back to Larkin. His tone was gentle.

"Tell it, boy. Tellin' it will help."

Britt told it, and it did help. He didn't feel so damned alone, now. These three quiet, good men beside him gave him something to lean on. He couldn't put it into words, but it was a mighty fine feeling.

They watched the cabin go to a pile of embers. Then Len Revis said, "We'll build the new one bigger an' better. I never was satisfied with the old one, anyhow. Not enough light when I was cookin' grub. Wonder I didn't use sugar for salt, half the time. Yes sir, we'll have a brand new roof over our heads before first storms come."

Banners of dust rolled up in several places across Reservation Valley. Rigs churned it up along the road from Fort Cord, rigs which carried Henry Castro and Hack Dinwiddie and Sam Garfield and his wife and several other solid citizens of town.

Then there was trail dust lifting behind Alec and Joyce Creager and Tom Adin and Race Wallace and Cotton Barr as they rode down out of the timber from Three Link headquarters. All were headed for the squatter camp on the flats. Here they found Len Revis and the Dodd brothers, Chuck and Harley. Here also they found an atmosphere of excitement and anticipation, tempered by some soberness and a quiet sorrow.

Those new to arrive heard for the first time the story of Sod Tremper's lonely death and they heard of the happenings up at Tin Cup headquarters. The telling of this last put a tired gravity on Alec Creager's face.

"It had to come," he said. "Why such things have to be, I don't know. Call it the stupidity men seem heir to. Yet, being realistic, it's for the best." He looked around. "Where is Britt?"

"Up at the dam with Oake Calloway," Len Revis said. "They're gettin' set to blow the lateral and let the water into the ditch." Len looked at Joyce Creager, who was big and still of eye and a little pale of face. "Time can do a mite of healin'. I've lived long enough to find that out. What's done is behind us. The future is made to live for. Now there's a girl who's sure lookin' at her future starry-eyed."

He pointed at Rose Calloway. Rose was in simple gingham, but it was starched and spotless. And she wore it like a queen.

"I — I don't understand, Len," said Joyce.

"Marriage comin' up," Len said. "Her and that young squatter, Cass Partee. Fine young couple. Country needs more like 'em."

Len was watching Joyce closely as he spoke. And now he saw soft color wipe the pallor from her cheeks and a warming moistness put a shine in her eyes. Len smiled with wise gentleness.

"Might be nice if you told Rose how happy you are for her," he suggested.

"Oh, I will," cried Joyce softly. "I will!"

Up in the gorge, Britt Larkin watched Oake Calloway set some final powder charges. The sturdy squatter turned to Larkin.

"These fuses you light, Britt. This whole thing was your idea. It's only right that you touch off what turns the water free. Have at it, boy. The folks down yonder are waiting."

So Larkin lit the fuses and they hurried off to a safe distance. It was all a little unreal to Larkin, at this final moment. Here an idea, what had once been almost a fantasy to him, now about to become fact. What had it cost? Plenty! What was its worth? Well, the future would tell that.

Again a hard, crackling thunder rolled along the gorge. Again a thin haze of rock dust lifted and fragments hurtled and bounced. Water in the lateral was whipped to dirty foam and pushed backward. But then it gathered force and swirled through where the last stubborn plug of rock had been. The first of it struck the long, curving gulch and the thirsty earth sucked it up. But there was more and ever more of it to flow past and downward.

In the valley people were grouped along the edge of the ditch which the Fresno scrapers had cut. From the mouth of the gorge Britt Larkin and Oake Calloway watched these waiting folk.

"Well, Britt, this is it," said Oake Calloway. "We'll let the folks down below get a good look at the water flowing in the big ditch, then we'll close the sluice gate and have our celebration. Sometimes I wonder if it's real. Then I look at the calluses on my hands and I know it is."

Britt nodded soberly. "And a cost to be

remembered, Oake."

Calloway knew what he meant. "A few give, many take. Jed Sharpe and Sod Tremper gave everything. They'll be remembered."

It took time for the water to sweep the full length of the gulch and then on into the man-made ditch. But the flow was full and strong and however much the earth drank up, it could not begin to take it all, and as the earth filled the rest swept by.

And so, finally, Britt and Oake could see rising excitement among the waiting groups, and they could see children running along beside the ditch and they knew the youngsters were racing the water flowing there. It was done.

When Oake Calloway spoke there was a husky note in his voice.

"We've traveled a long and weary road for this, but the journey ends here. I'm a happy man."

They looked at each other and shook hands.

After a while they lowered the sluice gate and the water flow dwindled and the gulch and ditch lay empty once more. But it would always fill again, when the need was there. The major task was finished.

Larkin and Calloway went down to the flats. There were handshakes all around and one of the firmest ones was between Alec Creager and Oake Calloway.

"I don't deserve this," said Creager gruffly. "Being allowed to watch this, I mean. I stand ashamed."

Calloway slapped him on the shoulder. "A man forms ideas as he goes along through life, Alec. In some he can be mistaken. But there's no harm done if he's big enough to admit it. That goes for both you and me."

Now a new note of excitement took over, this mainly among the women folk. There was much scurrying around and presently there was Cass Partee and Rose Calloway standing together before a traveling parson, a gaunt, towering man with deep eyes and a rolling voice.

Cass and Rose stood on earth that had been cleared by driving toil, under the open sky, and made their vows. It was a simple ceremony among simple folk, and their church was the whole bright, open world. Some of the women wept a little, but they were happy tears.

Afterwards there was feasting around the barbecue pit and men gathered here and there in little groups to talk of future plans and future building. And the afternoon ran away and the blue peace of twilight closed over the world.

Those who had come out from town sought their rigs and headed back. Three Link made ready to ride home. But before they left, Alec Creager sought out Britt Larkin.

"When you aimin' to start rebuildin', Britt?" he asked directly.

"Tomorrow, Alec," Larkin told him. "Fall's just around the corner. And sometimes an early storm hits. I aim to get ahead of that possibility."

"We'll be over to help," said Creager. "All of us."

Creager was good as his word. Three Link was there, not only on that day, but on all the succeeding days, while logs were cut and shaped and the walls of a new Tin Cup headquarters grew. Oake Calloway wanted to bring some of the squatter men up to help, but Britt Larkin would not hear it.

"You got building of your own to do, Oake. You can't ask your women folk to live another winter in their wagons. They've had enough of that."

Swinging an ax and running a saw from daylight to dark did things for Larkin, worked the darkness of spirit out of him. And then one day the change was complete. He and Len Revis were up on the new roof, adding the last row of split shakes. And Larkin found himself whistling. Old Len hunkered back and looked at him.

"About time you were comin' out of it," said the old rider. "You been the original gloom pot long enough. Get the hell out of here! I can finish with these shakes. Go on — go somewhere."

Startled, Larkin met Len's glance. "What do you mean? Go where?"

Len built a careful cigarette. "Go see your friends. Like the squatter folks, maybe. Let 'em know you've found out how to smile again. And it wouldn't hurt," added Len slyly, "if you rode over to Three Link. I can't remember you thankin' Alec Creager and his men for helpin' us put up the walls of this place. Yeah, long as you're over feelin' sorry for yourself, get out and spread a little cheer."

Larkin reached for Len's tobacco and papers. As he lit up, he grinned. "Think you're smart, don't you? Yeah, smart and smooth as all hell. Just as smooth as a bogged cow critter, wallowing in the mud. But as long as you're so ambiguous, go ahead and finish the job by yourself."

Larkin climbed down off the roof, caught and saddled. When he headed out, it was directly for Three Link. Len watched him go, grinning to himself.

"No idiot like a young idiot," remarked Len to the world at large. "He's been itchin' to go, and thought he wasn't showin' it. But he wasn't foolin' me none, not none at all."

There was a touch of fall in the air, a crispness which filled a man's lungs and speeded up the warm beat of his blood. There was a haze in the air which softened and mellowed the distance. It shrouded the high peaks of the Royales with a misty lavender and filled the timber with a smoky blue which became gold where the sun struck through.

Larkin, stung with a growing impatience, still rode slowly, savoring the world about him. He reined in for a time to watch a little bunch of his white faces graze across a grassy park. A little further on he stopped again, this time to watch a Douglas squirrel cut cones from a lofty conifer, then scurry down to earth to lug them away to hoard against the approaching days when winter would claim the land.

He crossed on to Three Link range and dropped down into the shallow gulch where the headwaters of Wagon Creek ran. And there he saw her. She was sitting on a mossy rock, watching the sliding water, dark here where the shadows struck, dappled with gold there where sunlight lanced down. Her horse, ground reined, stood patiently off to one side. She looked up quickly, startled at his approach.

Larkin splashed across, swung from his saddle. "I take it all back," he said.

She eyed him wonderingly. "I don't understand. Take what back?"

Larkin grinned. "What I said to Len Revis. The old son-of-a-gun must have double sight. How'd he know, Joyce, if I rode this way I'd bump into you?"

Her glance fell, settled on the water again. "Then you didn't come of your own accord? Len had to suggest it?"

"I came because I damn well wanted to," said Larkin quietly. "I didn't realize how badly I wanted to until I'd started."

He saw the color steal into her cheeks, though she kept her glance averted. "Be careful what you say, my friend. I — I might misunderstand you."

"No," said Larkin. "You're not going to misunderstand a word I say. And I'm meaning it, all of it. Like I never meant anything before in all my life. Look at me, girl!"

She stood up and looked at him, long and levelly, and great sweetness began to shine out of her.

"I needed a chance to forget some things, Joyce. There was a time when the man was a neighbor. We never did get along, Jesse and me, but he was a part of our world. I knew you'd remember that and I wasn't sure how you'd look at me, after —"

"How am I looking at you now, Britt?" she cut in softly.

He stepped closer to her. "And what do you see?"

"Just the two of us, Britt. Just you and me. We don't have to look back, Britt. It's our right to look only ahead."

He took her by the shoulders, gave her a little shake. "Not only very lovely, but very, very wise."

So now she was close and secure in his arms, and her lips the healing touch.

The employees of G.K. Hall hope you have enjoyed this Large Print book. All our Large Print titles are designed for easy reading, and all our books are made to last. Other G.K. Hall books are available at your library, through selected bookstores, or directly from us.

For information about titles, please call:

(800) 223-1244
(800) 223-6121

To share your comments, please write:

Publisher
G.K. Hall & Co.
295 Kennedy Memorial Drive
Waterville, ME 04901